"Undress me, El," Shane said as he grazed her breast with his fingers

"But we're *friends*." Maybe if Ella forced herself to remember that, she could back away.

"So maybe more friends should fool around," he said. His hand snaked down, teasing the soft skin on the inside of her thigh.

"Shane, I think—"

He cut her off with a kiss so long and deep, she was sure she was going to lose herself.

"Don't think," he said. "Let's finish what we've started."

Ella swallowed, but her fingers went to his jeans, fumbling with the button. Even though she knew she ought to stop this right now, somehow she couldn't. Somehow she *had* to have Shane. Now. Tonight. She wanted him inside her more than she could remember wanting anything before.

"Tonight doesn't really feel real, does it?" she whispered. "It's almost magical."

His lips brushed her ear. "There are always possibilities in the dark," he murmured. "And with a blackout..." When he trailed off, she looked up to see his wicked smile. "Well, the possibilities are endless."

Blaze™

Dear Reader,

Who wouldn't be intrigued by the thought of one day of passion? One day that makes all the difference in the world to two people? I definitely was, and when my editor approached me with the idea of writing a book that took place entirely within a twenty-four hour period, I jumped at the chance. And not long after the idea of "a twenty-four-hour book" registered in my head, Shane and Ella introduced themselves to me, along with the ever-popular question for a writer: What if…?

What if Shane and Ella were best friends? And what if one of them was keeping a secret? What if he wanted more than just friendship? And what if he was prepared to do just about anything—go to any erotic lengths necessary—to get what he wanted?

If all that happens over the course of one day (and one night!) you've got a story that's both fast paced and highly charged, and I couldn't wait to write it. Especially when I realized that Ella was friends with Veronica Archer (the heroine from *Silent Confessions*), and that adding a little Victorian erotica into the mix would spice things up considerably!

I hope you like Shane and Ella's story! I'd love to hear from you. You can contact me through my Web site, www.juliekenner.com.

Happy reading!

Julie Kenner

JULIE KENNER

Night Moves

HARLEQUIN®

TORONTO • NEW YORK • LONDON
AMSTERDAM • PARIS • SYDNEY • HAMBURG
STOCKHOLM • ATHENS • TOKYO • MILAN • MADRID
PRAGUE • WARSAW • BUDAPEST • AUCKLAND

ISBN 0-373-79198-4

NIGHT MOVES

Copyright © 2005 by Julia Beck Kenner.

This edition published by arrangement with Harlequin Books S.A.

® and TM are trademarks of the publisher. Trademarks indicated with ® are registered in the United States Patent and Trademark Office, the Canadian Trade Marks Office and in other countries.

www.eHarlequin.com

Printed in U.S.A.

1

As I touched her thighs, she put both hands down to stop me with a suppressed "oh," neither action nor word those of a woman who was shamming. It wasn't the fierceness of a girl who first feels a man's hand about her privates.... It was the exclamation and manner of a woman not accustomed to strange hands....

THE WORDS FLOWED OFF THE page of *My Secret Life,* sparking Ella's imagination and surrounding her with a haze of sensuality so thick and so hot that her pulse rate increased and breathing became an effort, like someone trying to suck in a deep breath in a sauna.

She'd been enrolled in the class for three weeks now and she still felt a jolt of excitement when she read a sensuous passage, little sparks deep down inside that made her wish for long nights with a determined man.

She'd never expected to be quite so intrigued by the words, although she'd signed up for Professor

Archer's class not only because of Veronica Archer's stellar reputation as an expert on erotica through the ages but also because Ella, frankly, needed to do something just a little wild. Just a little bit off the straight and narrow.

Not that she'd told Tony that. No, she'd told her boyfriend that she was taking the class out of loyalty and to investigate more fully her professional field. After all, she'd known Ronnie Archer for a few years now, and the two had become friends. So naturally she was curious about her friend's expertise. Plus, Ella was working toward her master's in art history, and Ronnie knew a lot about erotic art through the ages. So much that she'd been recruited to teach at the university in an adjunct capacity.

It was a reasonable explanation, and Tony hadn't batted an eye. It wasn't, however, an entirely true explanation.

The truth was, she'd seen something in Ronnie's work that she needed. Something that reminded her of her past. She used to drive fast cars and date fast men. She used to ride motorcycles along country roads with her best friend, Shane, or take a skydiving class just because he'd dared her to. Lately, though, she'd slowed down, the rough edges of her life smoothing out. She liked that, wanted it. But that didn't mean she'd erased the past—or that she didn't have the odd moment where she wanted to go a little crazy.

She smiled a little as she thought of Tony, with his clean-cut good looks and bank-officer wardrobe. While he'd indulge her with a night on the town to satisfy her wild streak, he was never comfortable with it. His sisters were another story, and when Tony was away or working, Ella and the girls sometimes went dancing or rock climbing or out to the track to rent and race fast cars. Fun, but not her life anymore. She was with Tony now, and unlike his sisters, Tony wanted a calm and orderly life. A family, with a picket fence and a dog—the whole nine yards.

And she wanted that with him, even though there were downsides.

For example, she'd tried twice to read him particularly enticing passages, but he'd managed to shift the subject, the mood, and very handily gotten her to drop the whole thing. Talking about sex, experimenting with sex—those weren't Tony's things.

Not that *sex* wasn't his thing. It was. The man was just fine in that department, if a little unimaginative. She loved him, though, and that made everything else balance. He was exactly what she wanted in a boyfriend. And, if she was reading the hints right, in a husband. Any day now she expected him to give her a ring, and she'd slip it on her finger without hesitation. Because Tony was everything she wanted, the man himself and his family. A big, boisterous, happy family. Exactly what she'd always dreamed of and never had.

Idly she flipped the page of the book in front of her, thinking how lucky she was to have Tony. She needed to get back to work, though, so she firmly pushed thoughts of her boyfriend from her head and forced herself to concentrate on the pages she was turning. Not difficult, since the lusty words caught her attention, pushing thoughts of her boyfriend from her head. In their place flooded erotic descriptions that had her imagination working overtime to bring her a vivid mental picture.

My, oh, my…

She leaned back in her chair, only half realizing that she was using a battered manila folder to fan herself. Usually her favorite study carrel in the back of the library was quite chilly. Today, however, it seemed remarkably warm.

I had drawn her near to me, was feeling all round her bum with one hand and wetting the finger of the other in her—

Wow.

How could anyone approach this from a purely academic angle? She certainly couldn't, at least not today. A particularly frustrating fact considering she was camped out in NYU library for the specific purpose of working on her term paper, or rather for the purpose of deciding the topic of her paper. She knew

she wanted to do something that juxtaposed historical erotica against modern works, but that was too
broad a topic. And as for brilliant plans to narrow her
theme, so far she was drawing a blank. Not good,
since she was due to meet with Ronnie on Monday
to go over the paper's thesis and outline.

Usually she was much better at focusing, but
today her mind had been all over the place. Maybe
because it was a stifling summer Saturday. Or maybe
because she'd already finished papers in the two
other classes she was taking this summer. She'd piled
on a killer course load, as usual, and the demanding
schedule was probably getting to her.

Not hardly.

The familiar voice in her head was her own, and
she knew exactly what it would say: she wasn't
cowed by a heavy workload. Deadlines and pressure
were what got her going. She was an adrenaline
jockey all the way, and had been all her life.

No, as much as she hated to admit it, her distrac-
tion wasn't caused by anything relating to her degree
program. The explanation was both simple and complicated: *Shane.*

He'd been her best friend for years, but now he
was abandoning her to move from Manhattan back
home to Texas, and she still hadn't quite gotten her
head around the fact that he was actually leaving.
He'd been in her life for as long as she could remem-

ber. They'd done elementary school together, and they'd split the cost of a U-Haul when they'd both come to New York as freshmen, thrilled to be escaping their equally nightmarish families and vowing to help each other through every ordeal the city might throw their way.

Seven years later, Shane had blown through college and law school and was now working as an assistant U.S. Attorney. Though just as ambitious, Ella was moving more slowly, with a degree in history completed and several credits under her belt that went toward her master's. She was determined to rack up the best academic qualifications. The kind that would get her a job at the Met—or, if her fantasies prevailed, the Louvre. She and Shane might have taken different paths, but they'd gone the distance together.

That he was now leaving wasn't something she liked to think about. A whole jumble of emotions kept washing over her. Hurt, anger, betrayal. They'd promised each other, but still he was going back. What made it worse was her certainty that Tony was going to propose. How was she supposed to plan a wedding without her best friend there for moral support? Although she had to admit that Shane might balk at that particular duty. She could occasionally talk him into crossing the threshold of Sephora with her, but Shane was a guy's guy. Wedding planning was probably a little too froufrou for his blood.

Still, she wanted him nearby. And she couldn't quite get her head around the fact that in two days he'd be outta here. That went against everything she believed in, most particularly her firm belief in happily ever after. Shane was part of hers, his friendship essential. And she hated the idea that they'd be nurturing that friendship across fifteen hundred miles.

She hated it, but there wasn't anything she could do about it. Lord knows she'd tried.

Part of her wished Monday would never come, so that he'd never leave. And part of her wished it were already next week, so he'd be long gone and her head could get back to focusing on her work.

Right. Her work.

As if beckoning, the pages fluttered in the breeze, stirred up by the makeshift fan she still held in her hand. Her gaze drifted back down, and the evocative language caught her attention once again.

Ella closed her eyes, her own imagination supplanting the words on the page. She wanted to pretend she was a total academic, interested in the language for its higher literary or scholarly significance.

A nice fantasy but not true.

Instead the language intrigued her, heated her blood just as she'd known it would. And made her wish she'd stayed in the privacy of her own apartment to study rather than coming to the library, where anyone who wandered into her dreary little corner might see her face and figure out *exactly* what was on her mind.

In the story, the man wasn't described at all. In her mind, though, he had dark hair, almost black. Tony's hair, of course, because who else would her imagination conjure? And although that hair could be smooth and debonair, at the moment it was tousled by her fingers, which ran through the coarse strands. A wilder Tony who existed only in her imagination.

His hands were rough, as if he occasionally worked with them, but not gnarled or calloused. They were strong and confident, and as she leaned her head back, his hands kneaded her breasts, his thumb and forefinger finding her nipple and rolling the soft nub between the pads of his fingers.

In her mind's eye, she arched back, hot wires of pleasure shooting from her breasts all the way down to her clit. He was there, between her thighs, the rough stubble on his cheeks scratching her sensitive skin as his tongue stroked her, a delicious counterpoint to the thrill of his hands on her flesh.

She couldn't see her lover's face. Just the dark hair on his head so intimately nestled between her legs, and the broad shoulders, muscles straining under his thin T-shirt as he stroked his hands down her belly, closer and closer to where his mouth was providing such wonderful attention.

She might not be able to see Tony, but she knew his touch. Strong. Confident. Just like the man himself.

Soon the pad of one thumb joined his tongue, and the added sensation sent her almost over the top. His other hand pressed on her lower belly, though, calming her and silently promising even more thrills if she was patient.

Oh, yeah. She could be patient....

She shifted just slightly in her chair, still half aware, thank goodness, that she was in a library and, though her mind might be going crazy, she had to keep her body under control. The devil between her legs shifted, as well, the brush of his cheek against her thigh sending a fresh wave of sparks swarming through her body. She almost moaned aloud, but her breath caught in her throat because right then his head lifted enough so that she could see his eyes— and they were *not* the deep brown of Tony's chocolate eyes.

These eyes were emerald green and all too familiar.

No. It couldn't be. There's no way *he* would be in her fantasies.

But then she could see his entire face, and there was no mistaking that fabulous jawline or that devil-may-care grin. She knew this man, all right. This man, with his tongue on her clit and his hands on her body. Oh, yes, she knew him well.

Shane! Her best friend. And a man who didn't belong within a hundred miles of her fantasies.

So what, she thought, was he doing there now?

THE APARTMENT WAS ONLY three hundred and fifty
square feet, and in a space that small the fumes were
making him giddy. At least, that's what Shane Walker
told himself as he unscrewed the last of the kitchen
cabinets so that he could take the doors out to the fire
escape to sand and stain.

The chemicals in the stain had to be getting to him.
There was no other explanation. Never mind that he
had all eight of the windows open and the fan in the
window unit going, and the vent over the stove going
and the ceiling fan chugging away at high speed.

Never mind that there was barely a hint of chem-
ical smell in the tiny apartment.

No, he *had* to be light-headed or giddy or something. Because if he wasn't, then what excuse did he
have for taking a break, settling himself in the middle
of Ella's floor and pawing through the box of old photographs and letters he'd found on the top shelf in the
kitchen, just behind the bottle of tequila with the actual worm inside? The bottle she kept but refused to
drink from, citing the ick factor of dead invertebrates.

But that's what he'd done not ten minutes ago, and
he felt like a total bastard for doing it. The pictures
in the box were tame enough. Pictures of him, of

Ella, of the two of them together. Boating, biking, hitchhiking from Houston to Mexico, hanging out on the boardwalk in Atlantic City. Souvenirs of the fun they used to have. None of their families, of course. No surprise there. But lots of pictures of their mutual friends. All no big deal.

And all of it none of his business.

He consoled himself with the knowledge that Ella would have happily let him look through the box if he'd asked. He knew she would. They'd been best friends since second grade, and there wasn't a request he could make that she would deny. For that matter, as far as he knew, there wasn't a single secret that Ella kept from him. He knew that her tortured relationship with her mom still gave her nightmares, waking her up in a cold sweat all too often. He knew she'd decided, so many years ago, to get a motorcycle license because she'd been surprised and aroused by the vibration between her legs when an old boyfriend had given her a lift home on his Ducati. And he knew that she'd enrolled in Ronnie's class on erotic fiction as much from prurient interest as from academic fascination.

They'd never actually voiced any plan to be so open; it had just happened as a natural growth of their friendship. By the time they'd reached college, they'd known pretty much everything about each other, from what type of birth control she used to which paralegal he'd fooled around with in the supply room at his first office Christmas party.

They knew everything, he thought, except the one secret that he kept from her. A big one. The biggest of the big. More to the point, the kind of secret that just might make her say no if he asked to look through the box behind the tequila.

But she didn't know his secret. He hadn't told her because he'd been too afraid the secret would screw up their friendship, and Shane hadn't been willing to run that risk. The truth was dangerous. The truth was hard and painful and wonderful all at the same time.

The truth was he loved Ella Davenport.

Looking back, he supposed he'd loved her from the first moment he'd seen her. Right there next to the slide in the playground at Sam Houston Elementary School. They'd both been seven, and he'd tripped and fallen, his very drippy Fudgsicle flying out of his hand. It had landed smack on her pretty pink dress and, unlike a lot of girls who would have yelled and cried, Ella had just laughed, brushed off the dress—making an even bigger smear—and offered to share her Eskimo Pie bar with him.

From that day Ella had become his best friend, his closest confidante. Never once had he thought of her as more than a friend, though. Not once in all those years in Texas.

Not once until about six months ago, when he'd

come home from a particularly bad date, called Ella on the phone to bitch about the so-when-will-you-join-a-big-law-firm-and-be-a-partner? bimbo he'd escorted to dinner and suddenly realized.

Ella.

The woman who'd been there in front of him all along. She was the woman for him. Absolutely and one hundred percent.

Not that he'd been able to tell her. Not then. The downside of knowing a woman as well as he knew Ella was that he was all too familiar with her quirks relating to relationships. If an ex-boyfriend said he really just wanted to be friends, no problem. But if the poor guy still had a boner for her—or, even worse, flat out said he was still in love with her—then once broken up, they were *really* broken up. She even went so far as to delete his entry from her Palm Pilot.

"Too awkward," she'd told him once. "Billy Crystal was only half right," she'd explained, referring to *When Harry Met Sally,* one of her favorite movies. "Guys and girls *can* be friends. Look at us. But only if sex and romantic love never enter the equation. If they do, every chance for happily ever after is shot to hell…" She'd trailed off, shaking her head, but he'd known what she'd meant. Ella's life hadn't been easy, and she'd survived the rough places by acting tough. Underneath it all, though, she was a cock-eyed optimist, absolutely certain that everything would be rainbows and sunshine in the end. Hell, maybe that's why she clung so fiercely to adventures like skydiving and rappelling—she innately believed that nothing could possibly go wrong, that the only possible outcome was a good one.

"God, can you imagine if we'd ever slept together?" she'd asked him during that same conversation. "How would I have lived without you in my life all these years?"

It had been a rhetorical question, and one he hadn't bothered answering. They'd never dated in high school or college, unless you counted the string of double dates, including a lot of dates-gone-bad where the two of them had ended up talking together in the bowling alley or on the dance floor while their respective dates had gotten plastered or flirted with someone else.

As the years passed, he dated often and sex was a given, of course. On occasion, he and El would get sloppy drunk and joke about going to bed, but they were never serious. They'd known each other for years—*years*—so why was he suddenly seeing her in a different light? Desperation born of the fact that he hadn't yet met another woman who could make him laugh as she did? Another woman he wanted to spend hours with watching late-night episodes of *Monty Python?*

No, it was more than that. Ella wasn't a last resort, she was his *only* resort. It had just taken him an ungodly amount of time to realize it.

And now—this week—he'd realized something else, too: he had to tell her. He had to risk everything and tell his best friend that he loved her.

Of course, a part of him believed that if he told Ella how he felt, it wouldn't be unrequited. Or, even if it was, that she'd put him in some stratosphere different from the other men in her life. *Him* she'd surely keep in the Palm Pilot.

Trouble was, he couldn't be sure. He couldn't imagine Ella ever shoving him out of her life. But things happened every day that he couldn't imagine. Like, for example, him moving back to Texas. Who would have thought after managing to escape the hellhole that had been his childhood that he'd willingly go back?

But here he was, two days shy of leaving New York to head back to Houston, Texas, to join a hand-picked Justice Department task force. A huge vote of confidence for a second-year attorney, especially when coupled with his superior's promise that if he did as well as they were expecting, he'd be transferred to D.C. once the task force disbanded.

Working for the U.S. Attorney's office in D.C. Now *that* was a gamble worth taking. He'd be a fool to walk away. And where his career was concerned, Shane was no fool.

About Ella, though…on that front, he'd admit to a little foolishness, especially lately. Foolishness with an edge, though. Foolishness with a plan.

For the past two years, he'd helped put away some of the nastiest criminals to face the Justice Department. He'd aced law review, interned for two federal judges and basically kicked butt where the law was concerned. He could plan, collect evidence and cross-examine a witness with the best of them. He might be raw, but he was getting better every day. Honing his skills, building his craft.

Now he was going to put those skills to work for personal reasons. He was going to tell her. Today. And he was going to prove to her that he was the man she belonged with, that she was his and always had been, even before either of them had realized it. He'd procrastinated for six months, but now he was on the verge of heading back to Texas. He couldn't wait any longer.

But it wasn't just the trip that was prodding him forward now. If that were it, he could take the coward's way out, fly to the new job, get settled, then fly back up to talk to Ella.

But there were other factors in play now. From what Ella had been saying recently, Tony was going to propose soon. And Shane couldn't lose her that way—not because some other man took her right out from under him. Especially when Tony was the wrong man for her. And Shane had no doubt that Tony was wrong. Ella was enamored, that much was true. But she was also trying too hard, smoothing out her own edges so that she could fit into the box that Tony expected her to fit into.

If, at the end of the day, she chose Tony, then so be it. But she needed to know all the facts. And the one big glaring fact was that Shane loved her. He wanted her. And they fitted together smoothly, perfectly without one alteration to her rough edges.

He knew that fact without a doubt, even as much as he knew that Ella might fight that simple truth. She had her reasons for wanting Tony, and he understood them. That understanding gave him an advantage, one he intended to use.

He glanced toward the kitchen, where he'd left his briefcase, smiling when he remembered what it contained. Not briefs and notes and legal memorandums, but still something he'd put all of his skill into creating. A little bit of demonstrative evidence for the plan he'd come to think of as Shane v. Tony, Judge Ella presiding.

He knew he might end up destroying their friendship. But he had to take the risk. Because, for the first time in their lives, another man might claim her for good. And Shane wasn't about to lose without even being in the game.

He'd win her over. He'd do it tonight.

Because in this game, Shane didn't intend to play fair.

2

ELLA PRESSED HER LEGS tightly together, determined not to let her imagination get the better of her. Were the fantasy about Tony—or anyone else, for that matter—she might have just gone with the flow. Even better, she might have headed home, drawn a hot bath, then lay naked on her bed and…

But this was Shane in her head, and he really had no business being there. More to the point, she had no business putting him there. He was her best friend, not her lover, and these wild thoughts were nothing more than the product of an active imagination. *Really.*

It took a more or less superhuman effort—and a Diet Coke from the machine on the first floor—but Ella managed to get her mind off Shane. Or, more to the point, off the vision of a hot and sweaty Shane who was doing absolutely delicious things to her body.

Her Shane wasn't dangerous. This imaginary Shane, however…

Ella let out a low, involuntary moan, hiding the reaction by taking the last swallow of soda, then tossing the can into the garbage. She headed back to her study carrel, her mind wandering back to her friend despite every effort to shift her thoughts to something less dangerous, like, say, nuclear holocaust.

No such luck, and with a sigh she gave in, accepting the fact that, for whatever reason, Shane was on her mind.

That wasn't even the problem, actually. He'd certainly been on her mind before. He was her best friend, after all. She thought about him all the time. But thoughts of a hot, naked, sexy Shane…a Shane whose rough fingers touched her and stroked her…

She shook her head, settling back into her seat. *That* Shane didn't belong in her thoughts. More importantly, she didn't know where the thoughts had come from. He was her friend. He had never even been on her nonplatonic radar. Not even one little bit.

They knew each other too well, too intimately, and nothing had ever once happened. In college, they'd slept over at each other's dorms, camped out in hotel rooms when they'd traveled back to Texas and been in every type of closed-quarter sort of situation. She'd never wanted to sleep with him.

Until today.

No, she corrected. She did *not* want to sleep with him. And even if she did—a teeny, tiny little bit—she wasn't stupid enough to go through with it. Shane was too important to her. And so, for that matter, was Tony.

Frustrated, Ella shoved her books aside, then rubbed her temples. As Saturdays went, this one was really not going well.

"I've got some Advil in my purse if you need it."

Ella jumped at the calm voice behind her laced with just a bit of humor. Veronica Archer, her professor for Lit 317, Erotica and the Victorian Society. And her friend.

When Ella spun around, she saw that Ronnie was smiling, and she returned the grin. Veronica Archer was stunningly beautiful and extremely self-assured, but she'd never seemed unapproachable.

"What are you doing among the stacks on a Saturday?"

"Looking for you, actually," Ronnie said. "I called your apartment and Shane told me you were camped out here working on a paper for my class."

"You talked to Shane?" Ella fought to keep her voice from squeaking.

"Like I said, he told me you were here."

"Oh."

Ronnie's brow furrowed and she looked over Ella's shoulder at the open page of text. A slow grin spread across her face. "Well, that explains why you looked so distracted when I walked up."

Ella snapped the book shut. "Don't tease me. I've got an academic interest only. You should know. It's your class I'm working on."

"I'm not teasing. I'm totally serious. You're the one who told me Tony's about to pop the question. Is it really that big a stretch to assume the direction your mind is going when reading erotica?"

"*Oh*. Right. Tony. Yes." She drew in a breath and told herself to just shut up because babbling really wasn't working for her.

"Weren't you—*oh*."

Ella closed her eyes and counted to five. "There's no 'oh' about it," she finally said when she looked Ronnie in the face again. "My mind was just wandering. That's all."

"To Shane," Ronnie said. She nodded sagely. "Interesting."

"Excuse me? What are you talking about?"

"Admit it," Ronnie retorted, "you were thinking about Shane when I came up. That explains that little catch in your voice."

"There was no—"

Ronnie shut her up with a wave of her hand.

"Fine. I was thinking about Shane," Ella admitted. "My best friend is packing up and moving fifteen hundred miles away from me. I've been thinking about him a lot." As soon as she spoke the words, relief flooded her. *Of course!* That's why she'd been lusting after Shane. It was so simple, any Psych 101 student would see it: she'd been feeling frustrated and angry when she couldn't beg and plead and force

Shane to stay in New York with her. So her subconscious was coming up with alternative methods of persuasion—seduction.

It wasn't lust. It was selfishness. Her id wanted Shane to stay in New York. Her psyche wanted its best friend.

What a relief. And thank goodness she'd taken that psych course, or she might never have realized the source of that absurd daydream. She and Shane, doing it like *that*. Doing it at all. The idea was ridiculous. Unthinkable.

And so damned appealing.

No! She sat up straighter, determined to keep her thoughts in check. "I'm just bummed that he's leaving," she said firmly. "That's all."

The teasing expression on Ronnie's face was replaced by one of genuine understanding. "I know, kid. He said he was heading out on Monday. You must be terribly sorry to see him go."

"Yeah," she said. "Yeah, I'll really miss him."

A beat, and Ella held her breath, wondering if Ronnie was going to shift the conversation back to erotica. Wondering even more if Ronnie was going to push for a more full description of Ella's recent fantasies.

But Ronnie simply nodded toward the exit. "Let's get a coffee. I have some news about your internship application."

And right then all thoughts of Shane evaporated. Ronnie had come here to talk about Ella's career, not her libido. And work was the one thing that never failed to snare Ella's full and complete attention.

ELLA STARED AT RONNIE over her coffee, not quite sure she comprehended what her friend was saying.

"I really got it? The internship at the Metropolitan Museum?"

Ronnie laughed and twirled the spoon in her coffee. "You really got it. I bumped into Dean Rostow earlier and he mentioned that he was going to tell you on Monday. I begged a little, and since I wrote one of your recommendation letters, he said I could go ahead and tell you if I saw you." Her smile widened. "So I've been searching the library for hours trying desperately to locate you."

"Thank you!" Ella flung her arms out across the table to hug her friend. The internship at the Metropolitan Museum—working directly with the curator—was both coveted and incredibly hard to obtain. Ella had been cultivating relationships, hoping for recommendations, since she'd been a freshman undergrad. She almost couldn't believe that her persistence had paid off.

"Why not?" Ronnie asked when Ella voiced the thought. "You worked much harder than all the other applicants. Why shouldn't it be you?"

"I don't know." She took a sip of her coffee. "I guess I still have a hard time believing how great everything has gone for me these past couple of years."

Ronnie's smile was kind. "Why shouldn't it go well? You work your tail off, don't you?"

"Hell, yes," Ella said. She nodded, the motion somehow boosting her confidence. "I deserve this, don't I?" Maybe life had been more difficult back in Texas, but that was why she'd left, right? So she could get away from the sorry life she'd had there and find a satisfying existence. She'd done it and she should be proud. And she was.

Ronnie put a hand over hers and squeezed, teacher and friend. "You *totally* deserve it."

"Wow." Ella shook her head, still not quite able to process the information. "Do you have any idea how good a stint like this is going to look on my résumé?"

Internships were highly competitive and depended significantly on who you knew. Ella's grades were stellar, but this was her first year in the program, which meant she was low on the totem pole. But that hadn't daunted her. She'd had her heart set on *two* internships since she'd entered the program—one for each summer of her master's studies. The field was extremely competitive. With two internships, her odds of finding a job that was both financially and emotionally rewarding increased significantly.

The ironic part, of course, was that her mother had

given her that bit of advice. As far as love, care and support went, Cecilia Davenport fell flat as a mother. But for career planning? Well, that was where Ella's mom truly shined.

She took a deep breath and laughed again, still overwhelmed by her good fortune. "Sorry. I'm just so excited. This is huge. I mean, an internship like this could lead to a job. Can you imagine? Working at the Metropolitan Museum fresh out of school?"

"If anyone can do it, you can. You're the most motivated student I've seen in a long time."

"You're just saying that because I make great margaritas."

"You're from Texas—you're supposed to be able to make all variety of drinks from tequila. And I'm not saying it because you ply me with alcohol. I'm saying that because it's true." She cocked her head and studied Ella. "Speaking of alcohol…we haven't had a wild night on the town in months. Probably since you and Tony started dating. But I guess you two have been having your own wild times."

"Yeah. Absolutely." She frowned and took a long swallow of her now-tepid coffee, ignoring the guilt and telling herself it was a fib, not a lie, and she didn't have to reveal all her personal details just because Ronnie was a good friend.

The truth was, she and Tony hadn't had sex in two weeks. During the workweek, their schedules never seemed to mesh, and the past weekend they'd gone out to his parents'. Ella had stayed up so late playing Trivial Pursuit with Tony's father and sisters that Tony had already been asleep in bed by the time she'd gotten back to their room. She'd thought about waking him but decided he needed the rest.

No more. Tired or not, he was going to have to come over the second he got off the plane from Los Angeles. And she'd even put on something sexy, like that itchy lacy thing he'd bought her for her birthday. She hated the thing, but she knew it would turn him on, and—

"Ella?"

She shook her head, pulling herself back into the conversation with a bright smile. "I guess both you and I have been having our wild times at home. That's the way it's supposed to be for you, right? After all, you're married now."

At that Ronnie laughed. "Jack doesn't mind if I go out drinking with the girls."

"He doesn't think you're being frivolous? Or worse, that you're checking out other guys?" The second the words were out of her mouth, Ella regretted them. Tony wasn't jealous and he didn't mind that much that she liked to go out with her friends. Not really. He just wanted her to stay with him, for them to enjoy their time together.

"I haven't been remotely interested in other guys since the first moment I laid eyes on him, and he knows it. But if I want to check out a few guys for my friends, he doesn't mind. He spends time with his buddies, too. Just because I got married doesn't mean I gave up my personality, you know?"

"Of course not," Ella said. "I didn't mean that. I just meant…" She trailed off. "I don't have any idea what I meant."

Ronnie leaned back in her chair, those penetrating eyes studying her. "What's bothering you, El?"

Ella ran her fingers through her hair. "Nothing, really."

"Yes, something. I didn't get to be a kick-ass professor for nothing. Now tell me."

Ella couldn't help but laugh. "I think it's just jitters, you know, about being engaged. I mean, I'm not even entirely certain he's going to pop the question—"

"Yes, you are. If anyone in this world is predictable, it's Tony. I don't mean that in a bad way, that's just who he is. You can see this proposal coming a mile away."

"Yeah, okay, you're right. I *am* sure. But marriage is something I really don't think I know how to do. It's not like I had a role model. It was just me growing up. Not even my mom. I want the family—I want all the trappings that go with a marriage—but I'm not sure how to *be* married. I've never really been a unit with anyone before. I guess I'm just a little nervous about how it works."

Ronnie's smile was soft and understanding. "Definitely jitters," she said. "As for how it works, it's a little bit different for everyone, but basically, marriage is about being yourself, only more. That's how it is with me and Jack. We're still totally ourselves, but we're a couple, too. It's nice." She reached out and touched Ella's arm. "And you *do* know how to be part of a unit. You do it automatically with your friends. Like me. And Shane."

The thought of being a "unit" with Shane almost undid Ella, particularly in light of her mind's earlier ramblings. "It's not the same," she said quickly. "I'm just myself around you guys."

"Yeah. That's the point." Ronnie studied her some more, and this time Ella ducked her head, uncomfortable with the inspection. "Isn't it? I mean, you're yourself with Tony, too, right?"

"Of course," Ella said. And she was. Everyone has different angles in their personality. Hers with Tony was more mature. Just the way it should be if she was going to be Tony's partner for life.

"Right," Ronnie said. She took a long sip of coffee, then played with the spoon for a while, clacking it irritatingly against the side of the cup.

"What?" Ella demanded.

Ronnie stopped, her hand frozen with the spoon. "Sorry. Nothing."

"Oh." Ella picked up her own spoon and tapped it silently against her palm.

"What?" Ronnie said.

Ella stopped the spoon. "Nothing. Really. I, um, just thought you had something more to say."

"No. Why? Is there something on your mind?"

"Okay, *fine*. You're going to keep bugging me until I spill it, so I might as well."

Ronnie kept her face perfectly placid, but her eyes danced with amusement.

Ella cursed silently, then spoke. "So, you and Jack, you're happy, right?" She knew they were. Blissful. Jack and Ronnie had snagged the happily ever after that Ella so wanted for herself. They didn't have kids yet, but she knew from conversations with Ronnie that little ones were on the agenda. It was perfect, and Ella was both thrilled for her friend and a tiny bit jealous.

"Very," Ronnie said, her forehead creasing in thought. She reached out and took Ella's hand. "What's on your mind, El?"

Ella took a deep breath, reminded herself that she'd opened the door and then jumped through it before she could change her mind. "Your, um, sex life is good, right? I mean, I know how y'all met and everything. It's not my business, but I'm assuming it's still really good."

During one of their margarita binges, Ronnie had told Ella the story of how she and Jack had met: there'd been a series of murders, and Jack, a detective, had come to Ronnie for expert advice about pieces of erotica the killer had been leaving at the scene. The attraction had been intense, one thing had led to another, and Ronnie and Jack had indulged in a few erotic fantasies of their own.

"It's wonderful," Ronnie said. She looked as if she might add something else but obviously decided against it, instead letting Ella go at her own pace.

"So, um, have you ever, you know, fantasized about another guy?"

"Ah," Ronnie said with an almost imperceptible nod, as if she'd just solved a huge mystery. She leaned back in her chair, then shook her head. "No, actually, I haven't."

"Oh," Ella said. Well, damn. So much for her theory that fantasies of Shane were just a normal little relationship bump.

"'Oh' is right," Ronnie said. "You're thinking about Shane." She made the statement firmly, without any hesitation. And for the first time Ella cursed having a friend who knew her so well. "When I came up to you earlier, you weren't thinking about Shane leaving at all, were you? You were thinking about all the interesting things you and he could do if he'd just stay here."

Ella briefly considered retreating into full denial, but the truth was, she couldn't. She needed to be open and honest. Shane might be her best friend, but Ronnie had filled the role of female friend in her life, and it felt nice. It also came in handy, because this was one thing she really couldn't talk to Shane about....

"Okay," she said. Then she drew in a breath and tried again. "Okay, yeah. Maybe." She slouched forward and let her forehead bang the table. "Oh, hell, Ronnie. What am I supposed to do now? I'm in love with Tony."

With major effort she gathered her emotions in, making sure nothing teary and weak would sneak out. Then she lifted her head just enough to peer at Ronnie. The sympathetic understanding on her friend's face almost unraveled all her hard work, and she had to double her effort to hold back tears.

"I'm a mess," she said. "I love Tony. He's great. The perfect eligible man. Good-looking with a great job and a real sense of humor. And his family loves me."

"You're right. He's a fabulous guy. His sisters are wonderful. It's a good thing, getting along with your in-laws."

"And I do. Really well." Already Ella had become great friends with Tony's two sisters, Leah and Matty, and his parents had welcomed her as if she were one of their own. With Tony she'd found the family she'd always wanted. With Tony she could have a perfect life. "This thing about Shane was an aberration. It had to be. Just my subconscious being bummed out about him moving so far away."

"Maybe. Or maybe there's something more. Maybe you should try and find out."

Ella stared at Ronnie, trying to comprehend what her friend was saying. "Are you nuts? No way. Just because I had a little fantasy about my best friend, that doesn't mean the sky is falling in. And it sure doesn't mean I'm not totally, one hundred percent in love with Tony. I have fantasies about Hugh Jackman, too, but I don't think we'll ever be like *that*."

"Why not?"

"Well, he lives in Los Angeles, for one thing. Or maybe London. I'm not quite sure."

Ronnie lifted an eyebrow. "*Shane,* Ella. I meant Shane."

"Aren't you listening to me? I already told you. I'm not interested in him. He's my best friend, not my personal sex toy. But these fantasies are really awkward. I mean, Shane and I have always talked about everything, but I'm sure not going to talk to him about this!"

"Maybe you should."

"Ronnie! I'm going to marry Tony. I love him."

"I know you do. But maybe it's not the right kind of love. Maybe he's not the one."

"Of course he is." She frowned. Of course Tony was the one. He had to be. She already had a life with him, a whole family who loved her.

"Well, you'd know," Ronnie said. "I just don't want you to let something special get away."

"That would be Tony, and you don't have to worry." She held up her hand, preventing Ronnie from saying anything else. "Look, I'm not denying that I had some pretty hot thoughts about Shane. But it makes total sense. I'm depressed he's moving back to Texas, and this is just my weird way of reacting to that. I don't *really* want to sleep with him."

"Well, maybe you're right," Ronnie said, but she'd edged back into her professorial voice, and Ella knew her friend was only humoring her. So much for girl talk. She should have just kept her mouth shut.

"Look," Ronnie finally said, "for the sake of argument, let's pretend you *do* want to sleep with him. Who's to say that very situation doesn't apply to him? Maybe he's desperate to sleep with you, but he's just as determined not to do anything about it."

"Oh, please." The idea was absurd. Never once had Ella picked up any clue from Shane, and they'd even shared a bed in the past. They were friends. True boy-girl friends. A relatively rare combination but not impossible.

"'Oh, please,' nothing," Ronnie countered. "You'll never know unless you try. So why not rush home, get him naked and have your wicked way with him?"

Ella fought the urge to bang her head against the table. Damn, but Ronnie was persistent. "One word—*Tony*."

She realized her mistake the second she said it,

and Ronnie realized it, too. A slow smile spread across her face. "So you're not saying you wouldn't want to go for it—it's just that Tony's standing in your way."

She shook her head vehemently. "No. No way. All right, maybe I'm a teensy bit curious about what it would be like to sleep with Shane—I mean, that makes sense, right? Me, girl. Him, boy. But I'm not about to go through with it."

"So we're right back at my question. Why not?"

"Because I couldn't stand my life if Shane wasn't part of it. And because I'm afraid of driving some sort of wedge between us. I mean, I saw *When Harry Met Sally*."

"So, instead of turning all Billy Crystal, you talk it out. Work through the whole thing. You guys are too close for something like sex to come between you. Even if it doesn't ultimately work out, all it will do is add an extra spin on your relationship. After all, you're both grown-ups, right?"

Were they? Sometimes Ella wasn't so sure. They'd pulled some pretty crazy, adolescent stunts in the past. Anyway, it was a moot point. Ronnie might believe in different spins, but Ella was afraid she'd be spun right out of Shane's life, centrifugal force shooting him fifteen hundred miles away, where it would be all too easy to forget to call and—frequent-flier miles notwithstanding—he'd be able to find all sorts of excuses not to travel between the states.

No, sex with Shane was a fantasy. Something that had popped in her head on a beautiful Saturday afternoon. And that's exactly where it should stay. In her head.

Out of sight. Out of mind. And absolutely, positively, out of her bed.

As SATURDAYS WENT, THIS one was supremely unproductive. And to make it even worse, Ella couldn't rush straight home, take a hot bath and hide from her troubles under five or six episodes of *Sex and the City* on DVD.

No, going home meant seeing Shane, and in her current frame of mind, she was afraid she might jump him or drool on him or do something equally stupid like tell him about the fantasy in the library. She desperately wanted to spend more time with him before he headed back to Houston, but right now wasn't the moment.

And so she did what every reasonable, intelligent, modern woman with a little time on her hands would do: she went shopping.

That was her favorite part about living in New York, actually. She could spend an entire day shopping and not spend any more than it cost to get a street pretzel and a Diet Coke.

She started by taking the subway to Fifty-ninth near the Plaza, then walking the length of Fifth Avenue, peering through the windows at all the fabulous bags and shoes. Things she wouldn't buy even if she had the money (twelve hundred dollars for a purse?) but were still fun to look at.

At about three o'clock, her cell phone rang. She checked caller ID, and when she saw Shane Mobile, a whole flock of butterflies seemed to take residence in her stomach. Great. Now not only was she in lust with her best friend, she was completely befuddled in his presence. Even his cellular presence.

She snapped open the phone. "Hey!" It sounded perky, cheery and not the least bit horny. One point for her team.

"Hey, yourself." The smile in his voice came over the phone lines loud and clear. "I've got your cabinets sanded and stained. They're drying on the fire escape, and they should probably stay there overnight."

"You're a saint, you know that, right?"

"That's me. Saint Walker." A pause, then he said, "So what time are you getting home? We could paint the bathroom together. I've got it masked off."

"Oh." She pictured the clothes she'd worn when they'd painted three of the walls two nights ago—a pair of cutoffs so short, she never wore them in public and a flimsy men's undershirt with the sleeves cut off. In the close quarters of her unventilated bathroom, the shirt would be sticking to her in no time, the shorts rubbing her in all sorts of provocative ways. And Shane would be right there, shirtless with a sheen of sweat, wearing those paint-splattered denim shorts that hugged his ass and—

"No."

"What?" He sounded confused. Well, no wonder.

"Sorry. I'm just a little stressed. This paper isn't going well. I was kind of thinking I'd stay at the library until late. Could I…I mean, could we take a rain check?"

"Sure thing, El." The silence on the phone dragged on, and then he cleared his throat. "Um, El?"

"Yeah?"

"You're not avoiding me, are you?"

Good Lord, was she that transparent? "Of course not. Why on earth would you say that? That's just ridiculous!" She closed her eyes, certain he could tell she was lying.

"Sorry. I just thought…well, I know you're mad at me for moving back and—"

"Oh, is that all?" She exhaled with relief, thrilled he was just worried about her temper and not her newfound lust. "Yes, I was mad, but I'm more sad. And I wouldn't sulk and let you leave without seeing you. That would be punishing both of us. But I have to finish this project. I'm down to the wire. Really."

"Right," he said. "Of course. So, I guess I'll just

head home now and get caught up on packing. How about we meet for breakfast tomorrow and then finish the job?"

Tomorrow. Surely she could get her libido under control by tomorrow. "Sure," she said. "That would be great."

"Good luck with the paper," he said, sounding like the good friend he was.

"Thanks. I'm sure I'll whip it into shape," she said, like the lustful, lying creature she was.

As soon as the line went dead, she snapped the phone closed, then looked around. She was standing in front of Crate and Barrel. Well, that would do.

Sometimes, though, window-shopping just didn't do the trick. And so she went inside to engage in a little bit of credit-card therapy.

SHANE STARED AT THE now-dead phone, more disappointed than he wanted to admit. It certainly wasn't Ella's fault that her paper was due right around the time that he was packing up to leave, but that didn't change the fact that he jealously guarded every minute they had together. He'd been secretly thrilled when she'd told him that Tony was in L.A. for business this week, since that meant even more minutes for Shane. But when time he thought was theirs was ripped away...well, he got a little pissed.

He wanted to get his plan underway. He was

pumped up and ready. And he didn't want to wait until the morning.

So do something about it.

He frowned at the thought. What was he supposed to do? She had to work and he had to pack.

After that, though…

He moved to the refrigerator and pulled out a soda, turning the thought over in his head. She hadn't suggested doing anything afterward, probably because she planned to work pretty late and expected to be tired when she finished.

But that was okay. He could work with tired and he could work with late. They could have dessert. Maybe even a whole dinner. A bottle of bubbly. And watch a movie on DVD.

A perfectly relaxing evening, brought to her courtesy of her best friend. A best friend who, if he played his cards right, would end the evening with Ella naked in his arms.

At least, that's what he was hoping for.

3

SLEEP WITH SHANE. THE idea kept skipping through Ella's head like a stone bouncing across the surface of a lake.

No, no, no, no. No!

She did not have to jump on every single impulse. That's what separated the humans from the animals, right?

During her four-hour shopping spree, she'd managed to spend only one dollar and sixty-three cents, the sum total for the chocolate bar and bottled water she'd picked up at a little bodega around the corner from Crate and Barrel. Her purchases—two hand-painted champagne flutes to add to her collection—didn't count since she'd bought them on credit.

Now, heading home with her book bag slung over her shoulder and her shopping bag in her hand, she had to fight the almost physical urge to go back out and shop some more. The cowardly woman's guide to relationship avoidance…

With a frustrated shake of her head she readjusted

her bags and headed down into the subway, pausing only briefly to consider crossing the street and taking the train to Shane's Upper East Side apartment. But no. She turned defiantly and headed for the train that would whisk her to the little studio she called home.

As much as she wanted to see Shane, it was probably better if she avoided him at least until tomorrow morning. By then, surely she would have wrangled her imagination back under control. Surely she'd be over this ridiculous desire to jump Shane's bones.

The train was mostly empty, and she grabbed a seat by a window, looking out toward the black nothingness as the train whizzed through the tunnels, the conductor's unintelligible voice announcing the various stops.

She let her mind wander and realized that, although she'd miss Shane when he moved back to Texas, maybe his leaving was for the best. She could manage one morning of keeping up a false front, but day after day? She was a grad student, not an actress.

That's right, she told herself. No need to be sad Shane was leaving. It was all for the best. The only way it could be better was if one of them was married. She thought of Tony and smiled. Maybe soon she would be. And her libido would be aimed at only one man. Tony.

As soon as she had a ring on her finger, there

would be no question about the parameters of her relationship with Shane. They'd be friends.

And absolutely nothing more.

THE FRIENDS-ONLY PLAN WAS firmly in her mind twenty minutes later as she stood in front of her door, busily attacking the three dead bolts that kept the world out of the inside of her apartment. When they were finally unlatched, she turned the knob, leaned her hip against the apartment door and shoved, urging the sticky door open.

When she first opened the door and saw him, she didn't believe her eyes. Shane wasn't supposed to be there. It had to be an illusion brought on by a Shane-filled brain.

But it was him, all right. Shane Walker, standing there in a crisp white shirt knotted at the neck with a tie she'd given him two birthdays ago. He wore a pair of snug jeans that showed off his perfect rear, and when he saw her, he held up a deep red rose. And for just a moment the heat in his eyes matched the fiery red of the petals.

No. She had to be imagining that. And when she blinked and looked again, it was just Shane, his expression decidedly pleased and self-satisfied, but this time there was nothing heated in his eyes.

Was that disappointment she felt? No, it couldn't possibly be. Curiosity, maybe. Yeah. That's all. She took a tentative step into the apartment. "What are you doing here?"

"Come on in and see."

She squinted at him, then moved farther inside, her steps taking her beyond the trifold screen she'd bought off eBay six months ago. Shane had been standing just beside it, so she'd been able to see him, but her tiny table had been blocked by the screen, which formed a makeshift dining room-cum-office in the small apartment.

Now she could see her table. This morning it had been piled high with books. Stacks of erotic literature. Various cataloging manuals and piles of art history texts. And the latest J.D. Robb, which she kept as a reward for when she got enough schoolwork done.

Now the books were gone. The usually scratched tabletop was covered with a white linen tablecloth. Two place settings in a china Ella didn't recognize took up most of the tabletop. Shane placed the rose in a slim vase in the center. A bottle of champagne was chilling in a bucket next to the table. Champagne was Ella's secret vice, and her eyes widened with surprise.

"What is all this?"

"I thought you could use a relaxing evening. And I wanted to buy you dinner before I went away."

"Buy?"

He nodded toward the tiny kitchen, and she saw the

stacks of white boxes and round foil containers. "Craft," he said, referring to Ella's favorite restaurant and one of the hottest dining establishments in the city.

"You got Craft *to go?*"

He laughed. "My boss knows one of the chefs. I called in a favor and he said to call it my 'kick butt in Texas' present."

She couldn't help her smile. "They know what a prize they got when you picked Uncle Sam over some big law firm. I bet everyone is sorry to see you go—and jealous they're not on the task force, too."

"There's a little envy," he admitted. "And there are definite downsides to leaving, even if it is the biggest opportunity of my life. But you know I couldn't not take it."

"I know." And she did. They were too much alike for her not to understand. In a way, ambition defined them. And, in a way, ambition had raised them. Certainly their parents hadn't bothered to do the job. Instead they'd both reached for something else, something to give them an identity other than an accident of birth. They were each determined to make themselves.

It didn't take a pop-psychology class to get to the heart of it. Ella knew that both her academic drive and her need for a cohesive family stemmed from her pathetic childhood. She knew it, she understood it and she wouldn't change it.

Just as she wouldn't change Shane's ambition. It was part of who he was. And although she was sad about him leaving, she knew too well what he'd be giving up if he stayed. Almost as much as she'd be giving up if she took Ronnie's suggestion and walked away from the life she could have with Tony.

She glanced again around her apartment. The shock of seeing Shane had worn off, replaced by the realization that she'd eaten next to nothing today. "Dinner, huh?"

"I may be leaving on Monday, but in the meantime, I thought we could stuff ourselves silly and then kick back on the couch and watch…" He trailed off, turning slightly to rummage behind him as Ella looked on, amused.

Finally he turned back, this time with a DVD case from Blockbuster. He handed it to her. Their fingers brushed as she took the case, and any illusions that Ella might have had that she'd be able to keep this sudden lust thing under control dissolved under the force of the sparks shooting through her fingers. Damn it all and damn Ronnie. Those books were making Ella a basket case.

She looked down, sure her cheeks were flaming, and concentrated on opening the box. When she did, though, her discomfiture faded, replaced by a burst of genuine laughter when she saw what was inside: *Monty Python and the Holy Grail.* One of her favorite movies, and one that she and Shane had seen over and over and over.

"How ever did you know?"

"I'm just a perceptive kind of guy," he said.

"I guess so," she murmured. But she wasn't really thinking about her words. She'd moved closer to him to take the DVD, but now the movie was the last thing on her mind. His scent filled her head. *Kouros.* A cologne he'd worn every day for at least a decade. She was as familiar with the musky scent as she was with Shane himself. So why did both seem so new right now? New and heady and unbelievably sensual?

And the way he looked…

When she'd left the apartment this morning, he'd been decked out in denim shorts and a thin gray muscle shirt. The outfit had accentuated his rugged good looks, decidedly *un*lawyerly. If she'd snapped a Polaroid of him before she'd walked out the door, she had no doubt he could make the cover of any calendar of sexy men.

It had been that image of masculine virility that had spawned her fantasies in the library, and any suggestion that Shane might look even more sexy fully clothed would have seemed preposterous.

Now, though, Ella knew it wasn't preposterous at all.

He was freshly shaved, his thick hair combed back with just a bit of gel, but that one unruly strand still fell across his forehead, brushing the top of his dark eyebrows. His jawline formed a rugged angle that almost screamed for her to reach out and stroke it.

Even his tie was sexy, all the more so since she knew the broad chest it lay against, as well as the rugged, muscled abdomen she'd reveal if her fingers loosened that tie and went to work on those buttons.

And his butt! Good Lord, it really should be a crime the way his ass filled out the tight denim.

"Ella? *Ella!*"

Her name seemed to cut through some fog in her brain and she blinked. "What? I'm here. What?"

The look he shot her was filled with amusement. "I went into the kitchen to check on the stuff warming in the oven and you went comatose on me. What's on your mind?"

"Nothing!" Then she added, "Nothing. Really. Just school stuff. I guess I'm still winding down."

"Well, hurry up with that. We don't have that much more time before I'm out of here. I don't want to share you with Ronnie or any of your other professors tonight."

"Right. Sure."

"And thank God Tony's out of town this week, or I swear I'd have to arm wrestle him for the chance to hang out with you before I left."

She smiled and shrugged. Tony and Shane got along okay on the surface, but neither one of them would have been thrilled by the idea of all three of them hanging out together. *Under* the surface, there was some definite tension.

"Do you want to change? Dinner's just about ready."

She nodded, mute, then turned to the armoire that doubled as a television stand and closet. She grabbed a pair of yoga pants and a cotton tank top. As she headed into the tiny bathroom, she wasn't really thinking about changing clothes, though. And even though she knew she should be, she wasn't thinking about Tony either. Instead her thoughts had drifted back to her conversation with Ronnie.

Sleep with Shane?

The thought, which she'd earlier examined fairly objectively from a psychological perspective, now held real, solid appeal. A terrifying amount of appeal, actually, and she wondered if maybe she should just—

Stop it, Ella. Just stop it.

And besides, there wasn't any risk that her little blip of desire was reciprocated. Ella had been sincere in what she'd told Ronnie—Shane had never once made a pass or even looked as if he might make a pass. The closest, in fact, was tonight. That heat she'd seen in his eyes…

As she changed clothes, she told herself that she must have been imagining things.

No lust, no attraction, she told herself. *Just dinner with your best friend. Same as you've done a hundred zillion times.*

Ella had taken a single drama class back in high school, and the teacher had been a big fan of improvisation. For the most part, Ella had sleepwalked through the course. She had no interest in being an actress and even less in pretending to be a monkey at the zoo or a woman trapped in a subway or a little kid not picked for the kick-ball team (who thinks up those stupid scenarios anyway?). Now, though, she was wishing she'd paid a bit more attention to technique. At the very least, she was wishing she had a bit more raw dramatic ability.

The voice in her head shifted from her own to Miss McNally's nasal lilt. *Remember, Ella, you must hide everything. Close off all emotion except what you want your audience to see. Okay,* go!

Ella jumped at the command in her imagined instructor's voice, her hand turning the knob and pushing open the bathroom door before she had any more time to think. In the apartment, Shane looked up, a match in his hand.

"So what do you think?"

Candlelight? He expected them to dine by candlelight? Candlelight fueled lust. He wasn't playing fair. He wasn't—

She frowned. He wasn't playing at all. Shane had no idea about the thoughts running through her head. If he wanted to set a fancy table, then great. Wonderful. What a thrill.

"Looks spectacular," she said, taking some pride in the fact that her voice didn't shake.

"Like I said, I wanted to go all out. Especially with your birthday in a few weeks. This will be the first time I've missed it in, well, forever."

"Oh. Right." Well, damn. She realized with a start that a tiny bit of her had actually hoped he was making some sort of romantic gesture. The mention of her birthday dinner, however, squashed that hope like a bug.

Ever since they moved to New York together, they'd taken turns treating each other to amazing birthday dinners. If one of them had an actual date on their birthday, the dinner was moved to a nearby evening, but they never failed to get together. It was fun, it was tradition and it was a chance to splurge on fabulous food guilt-free. After all, you couldn't feel guilty about buying your best friend a birthday dinner, even if you were near your limit on your Visa card and had yet to buy textbooks. Friends came first, right?

"So, if this is my birthday dinner," she joked, "does that mean I've got a present, too?"

He chuckled, then pulled out her chair for her. "Sorry, kid. I'm not that organized." He moved to the other side of the table and took his seat, the corner of his mouth quirking in a familiar grin. "But you can tell me if there's something in particular you want."

Was it her imagination, or was his voice deliberately pitched low? She swallowed as the butterflies in her stomach took flight and her mind ran over all the possible "presents" he could offer. *Oh my.*

Her breath hitched, and it was all she could do to fight the urge to scream, "Yes, yes, I want *you.* I want a wild, stupid fling." Except, of course, she didn't want that. Couldn't want that.

Damn. She really was a mess. And tonight—when her unexpected fantasy was so fresh on her mind— was the worst possible night to be spending with him.

Calling on intense self-control, she managed a simple shrug as she picked up her salad fork. "I've got one or two things in mind," she said. And although she tried desperately to keep her tone flat and in control, she was appalled to hear the hint of heat that crept into her voice. Which probably went a long way to explaining why she'd gotten that C in drama and blown her straight-A average.

"Are you going to tell me?"

She shook her head, probably a little too vigorously. "I don't think so."

He perked up at that. "No? Hmm. So I have to guess. That's okay. I'm a good guesser." He grinned. "Besides, right now I know exactly what you want."

She felt her eyes widen, and despite her best effort, her voice came out squeaky. "You do?"

"Absolutely," he said. "And you can have it."

"I—I can?" A bead of sweat trickled down between her breasts, and Ella swallowed, trying to will her body back to a place of calmness and serenity.

Not hardly.

He picked up the open bottle of champagne. "Birthday bash, remember? I figure we can go a little wild."

Ella clenched her fists at her side, stifling an overwhelming sigh of relief. "Right. Champagne. Great."

His eyebrows drew together, and he looked at her the way he might look at a hostile witness. "What did you think I was going to say?"

"Nothing. I'm sorry." She waved a hand, even more seriously regretting that C. "I'm just stressed about that paper. And, you know, sad that you're moving."

"Just sad?"

She nodded. "I'm over being pissed off. I mean, it's your career. That's the one thing I truly understand." And it was true, too. She *did* understand why he was going. But it still hurt all the same.

She shook her head to clear it. "So, you've really done it up, huh?" She took in the table, really seeing it for the first time, and not just the trappings. He'd returned the champagne to the table without pouring it, and now she saw the label. "This salad is amazing. And is that Cristal? Wow. You splurged."

"For you? Anything."

"Especially since you get to split the bottle."

"There are three bottles, actually. I bought you a couple of extras." He flashed a lopsided grin. "We can finish them off tonight, or you can keep them around to remember me by."

"Just the thought depresses me."

"In that case," he said, "I really need to pour you this drink."

"Can't argue with that." She started to lift her glass, then remembered her purchases. "Wait a second." She ran to her bag and unwrapped the flutes, then held them up with a flourish. "Ta-da!"

As expected, Shane laughed. "You can never be too rich—"

"Or too thin or have too many champagne flutes," she continued, finishing the line she'd said so many times to him—every time she'd splurged on another flute for her collection.

"So I've been told," he said. "Serendipity, huh? I mean, you buy yet another pair of flutes, and I bought champagne. We're like champagne and caviar. We go together."

She managed a watery smile as she held up her glass. "Fill it to the brim," she insisted. "I can use it."

He leaned over to do just that, and as he reached toward her, she noticed him wince. Pain flashed in his eyes as he held the bottle steady, and she could see that he was fighting a grimace. When he pulled back and set the bottle on the table, his face cleared, and she could almost hear his sigh of relief.

"You want to tell me what that was about?" she demanded.

"Nothing," he said. He rolled his right shoulder, wincing again as he did so.

"It's not nothing," she said, frowning. Back when she and Shane were in junior high, Shane had caught a ride home one stormy afternoon with his older brother, Marc. Marc had been driving too fast, lost control on a curve and flipped the car. Marc had been killed instantly. Shane had been banged up pretty good, the only enduring injury being a shoulder that tended to get pulled out of whack way too often.

There'd been emotional injuries, of course, and she and Shane had leaned on each other even more. Since neither had a solid family to rely on, they'd become each other's family.

A wash of memory swept over Ella, bringing in vivid color to her mind the first time she'd really let Shane in on the horror of her life. They'd lived in an affluent enough section of town, and though her parents were divorced, both were Important People, doing the social and political thing. But they hadn't done the parenting thing. Her father had just flat-out ignored her—she'd seen him a grand total of twice since the divorce. And her mother had used the excuse of having to work, then dumped Ella with the maid. All that even though Cecilia Davenport had enough money in oil royalties never to work a day in her life.

Considering her mom's attitude, Ella hadn't much minded spending the day playing with the maid's daughter. Not an ideal life, but she could have dealt with it had the worst not happened.

She'd gone to a fund-raiser for some society thing her mom had been working on. It had been held in the summer at the estate of one of the society members. Tommy McQueen, Central High School's star quarterback, had been there. The few kids present had hung out by the pool. Tommy had flirted with her, although she'd been too shy to flirt back, especially since she'd been a lowly freshman. But when she'd tried to escape to the safety of the inside, he'd pulled her aside, then dragged her into the pool house. As she'd fought, he'd fondled and almost raped her, coming so close, she'd had to endure the humiliation of a rape kit.

She'd managed to get away, though. And she could still remember the shocked looks when she'd told who'd done that to her. *Not a football player! It couldn't be!* In Texas, football was magic and power, and in addition to being a local celebrity, Tommy had powerful parents.

Her parents had refused to let her press charges, fearing that somehow their own careers would be damaged. For this humiliation, her father actually had gotten involved, though the rat bastard had never once come to see how Ella was doing. The police, without a witness and who were probably huge fans of Central's winning season, had dropped the case.

Ella had hated her parents for that, acknowledging for the first time what she'd already known in her heart—she wasn't their priority. She wasn't even close.

In the end, she'd hated the town, too. Too many bad memories and too few good ones. Shane, in fact, had pretty much marked the parameters of what had been positive in her life.

She knew he felt the same. His family had been poor, his mom a drunk and his dad verbally abusive. Neither worked a steady job, and it was astounding that Shane had such a great smile considering he hadn't even gone to a dentist until high school.

Shane's brother had been a slacker but kind—and Shane had been devastated when he'd died. When Marc died, so did everything good in their family for Shane.

Junior high had been a tough few years. *That* was an understatement. But they'd gotten through it together.

With a sigh Ella shook off the memories. She was in New York now and life was good. And even if Shane was going back to Houston, it would be different for him now. He was going on his own terms, with his own life. She didn't need to worry about him.

But she was worried about that shoulder. She got up, then moved around the table, coming to stand behind him. "Did you pull it out again?"

"Yeah, but it's really not bad. Just a little sore."

"Dammit, Shane! This happened because you were painting my apartment, didn't it? I told you I didn't want you to do anything that might screw up your shoulder."

"It's fine," he said.

She scowled, irritated that he'd hurt himself working for her and feeling completely responsible. "It's not fine," she said. "I can see it's not fine."

"Okay," he said, flashing that grin again. "You're right. It hurts like hell. But it was a small price to pay."

"For what?" she asked, incredulous.

"For that," he said, waving an idle hand toward her fire escape.

Curious, she got up and crossed the short distance to the window. The double-pane glass had long ago fogged over, so she unlocked it, threw up the sash and poked her head outside. There, drying on the metal grating, were her kitchen cabinets.

"Wow," she said. And then, because that hadn't conveyed the right tone, she added, *"Wow."*

"Not bad, huh?" he asked, coming to stand behind her.

"Not bad at all," she breathed. He'd done an amazing job. The cabinets—previously clumpy and thick with layer after layer of paint accumulated over the years—had been completely stripped down to the wood. And what Ella had assumed was cheap pine turned out to be some fancy hardwood, complete with an amazing wood-grain pattern. Shane had stained each piece, and the effect drew the grain out even more, emphasizing the natural beauty of the wood.

The sun had already disappeared behind the taller buildings that surrounded Ella's apartment, so she stepped outside and flipped on the little light that she'd rigged up for the fire escape. In the dim illumination provided by the single bulb, the wood seemed to gleam. She moved forward, approaching one of the cabinet doors.

She reached out a finger, then hesitated. The raw beauty of the wood called to her, and she wanted to stroke it, but she didn't want to mar any of Shane's hard work.

Shane. She realized with a start that he'd come up behind her. He was standing there, his breath on the back of her neck, the toe of his shoe pressed against the heel of hers. His hips weren't touching hers, but she knew he was back there. Knew that all she had to do was take one tiny step back and her rear would be pressed right there, right against him.

Good God, what was wrong *with her?*

"Go ahead," he said. "Touch it."

"What?" Her voice came out raw, so she cleared her throat and tried again. "What did you say?"

"The cabinet door," he said—and was that amusement she heard in his voice? It couldn't be. He couldn't know what she was thinking.

"The door," she repeated stupidly.

"If you keep holding your finger out like that," he said, "a bird is going to land on it."

"Oh. Right." She quickly dropped her hand.

"Touch it," he insisted, his voice sounding low and erotic, even though she now realized he was talking about the door. "You know you want to."

"I don't want to mess up your work."

"It's dry."

"Really?" Not quite believing him, she inched her finger closer until finally she ran the tip down the smooth lacquered surface. Just as he'd said: dry.

He chuckled, his breath tickling the hair on the back of her neck. Never in her life could she remember having been so aware of Shane.

"I told you."

"You did a great job." She drew in a breath. "These are absolutely beautiful."

"Thanks." He moved to stand beside her. "I wanted to finish this up for you before I went away."

She couldn't help her smile. "Yeah? I thought you were the one who was supposed to get a going-away present. Not the one who's staying behind."

"You know me. I like to be different."

"Well, um, thanks again." An awkwardness settled over her, and she realized that on any other day she would have brushed his cheek with a kiss. Today, though, she couldn't bring herself to do it, too afraid of where the kiss might lead. Or maybe afraid that it wouldn't lead anywhere at all.

If Shane realized her discomfiture, though, he didn't show it. Instead he bent toward the nearest cabinet door. "Shall we take them inside?"

"Is it okay?"

"Sure," he said, but as he lifted it, she saw him wince.

"Whoa, whoa, whoa," she said. "Down." She pointed toward the grating. "Put it back down now."

He just stopped and held it in front of her, his brow furrowed.

"Now," she said, stabbing the air with her finger. "Right there."

"Ella..." Reprobation laced his voice, but he didn't argue. And when he stood back up again, she made a circle motion with her finger. "Turn," she ordered.

Fortunately Shane was more than familiar with her no-nonsense voice and he did as he was told.

"What were you thinking?" she demanded, moving closer. "I specifically told you not to do anything that would screw your shoulder up again."

"I didn't—"

"Don't even start," she said. She pressed her hands

against his shoulders, something she'd done hundreds—no, thousands—of times during their friendship. This time, though, the contact sparked electricity, and a million volts shot through her fingers and ricocheted through her body.

With a little yelp she yanked her hands back, suddenly aware that her nipples were hard and her crotch warm. *Shit.*

"El?"

"Sorry. Just, um, static electricity. I'm fine."

She swallowed, took a deep breath and tried again. This time she managed to touch him without sparking a flood of lascivious thoughts. She drew a breath and kneaded his flesh, paying special attention to the knot she felt just under his shoulder blade.

He exhaled, a sigh of pleasure on his breath. "Oh, yeah. Thanks. That feels awesome."

She squeezed her eyes tight, glad he couldn't see her face. This had been a very, very, *very* bad idea. She should have called her house first. Should have gone out of her way to make sure he was nowhere in the vicinity before she'd come home.

No way should she have walked through those doors and been forced to face Shane mere hours from the time her mind had started conjuring images of her and Shane in a variety of acrobatic, erotic and decidedly naked positions.

Well, maybe she'd made a mistake coming, but

she fully intended to rectify that error right now. She would very calmly tell him that her head was throbbing and that she really needed just to lie down and take a nap. She'd suggest they meet for breakfast, he'd leave, she'd take a cold shower and by morning she'd have her head, her body and her libido under control.

Yes. That was a good plan. A plan she could live with.

But then Shane said, "That's enough, thanks," and started to turn in her arms. And that was when Ella realized just how wrong even the best of plans could go.

"I—" He was right there, his face so close to hers, his lips slightly parted. His green eyes were warm and they seemed to pull her inside them. She wanted to go. She wanted to lose herself in those eyes. The eyes of a lover and of a friend.

And before she could think, consider, talk herself out of it, she inched forward, her mouth tingling with the mere possibility of a single forbidden kiss.

Snap!

Ella jerked back, her breath coming fast as she realized that every light in the city had been extinguished, as though God had simply blown out the candle. She stood there for a second, disoriented by the pudding-thick blackness.

And then she said a silent thank-you to the powers that be, whether divine or merely ConEd. One of

New York's famous blackouts had saved her from embarrassing herself with Shane.

Fate, she thought, was watching out for her.

4

"El?" SHANE REACHED OUT instinctively, needing to find her in the black, but his fingers found nothing but air. "El?" he repeated.

"I'm fine. Fine," she said, her voice unnaturally high.

"You sure?"

"Absolutely. Of course. Just startled. Probably a power surge. This heat has got to have all the air conditioners working overtime."

"Probably right." Something in the back of his head said that he ought to get inside and start fumbling around for flashlights and candles. But he couldn't seem to get the synapses in his head to send the message to his limbs. Instead, he was rooted to the spot, his mind turning over one question and one question only: *Had Ella really been about to kiss him?*

No way.

That was impossible. Totally unthinkable. Unprecedented. Absolutely not true.

And yet…

There *had* been something in her eyes. A spark of interest. A hint of heat. Just a tiny indication that she was longing for him as much as he was longing for her.

But no, surely he was mistaken. The heat he'd seen in her eyes was just a reflection of his own prurient thoughts. Because that's what his thoughts had been. Dark and needy and filled with lust.

The moment she'd touched him, it had been as if she'd turned on a movie in his mind. A close shot first, of her hands on his shoulders. Then the camera pulled back to reveal her face, eyes closed as her fingers kneaded his tender flesh. Her expression was one of seductive ecstasy, and he felt his cock stiffen with the memory of that fantasy.

In his mind, she slipped her hands down his front, and she'd stepped up closer behind him so that her hips fit against his as her fingers went to work on the buttons of his shirt.

She then abandoned the cause of his shoulders, her warm hands instead finding new fascination with his chest as she stroked and teased and he grew harder and harder, his entire body filled with a desperate longing for her, a lust and a need so urgent, he thought he would explode if he couldn't have her right then, right there.

He'd spun around under her touch, and the fantasy had miraculously become real. At least a little bit. Her hands hadn't really been stroking his chest and her hips were well away from his—a little fact that, in retrospect, was probably good, because there was no way he could have hidden his massive hard-on from her.

But her face had done him in. That expression of need and want and longing. Longing for him. And, he was certain, the promise of a kiss.

You're insane, he told himself. He knew perfectly well he was deluding himself if he thought she could want his fantasy movie to become a reality.

Fantasy and reality weren't the same. He knew that. He was a lawyer. He dealt in facts and evidence and persuasion. Before the night was over, he intended to lay his case out in front of Ella and persuade her to his side. That was his intent, anyway. And Shane had yet to pursue a losing case.

"Shane? Did you hear me?"

Her soft voice pulled him out of his reverie.

"What? Sorry. What?" he asked.

"So what do you think happened? Just a blackout, right?" Her voice sounded oddly stilted, as if she were working to make conversation.

"That's what I'm thinking. Probably a system overload, just as you said."

He realized with mild surprise that he could actually see her face now, though *see* was probably too strong a word. Rather, he could make out the subtle lines and contours and discern a hint of expression. The night was overcast and there was no moon, so this sudden glimpse surprised him until he glanced around and realized the source of the illumination: hundreds of candles and flashlights filling the dozens of windows that surrounded Ella's apartment.

While he'd been busy fantasizing, their neighbors had been busy working the situation, and now the city was lit by the warm, barely existent glow of candlelight. He pointed off the balcony, fairly certain she could see the shadow of his arm and the direction he was pointing. "Look," he said.

He watched her face, his heart lifting when the shadow of her mouth shifted into a tiny smile.

"Well," she said, "if nothing else, it's pretty."

"Come on. Let's get inside and turn on a radio." He moved toward her, planning to take her arm and maneuver the two of them through the dark into the apartment. She twisted sideways, though, managing to avoid his grasp.

"You go ahead," she said. "I'll follow."

He stared at her for a moment, trying to read her expression, but the light was too poor. Was she simply, innocently, wanting to walk unassisted? Had she picked up on his überlust?

He considered the possibilities as he picked his way back to the window, careful not to step on the cans and brushes still outside drying. He could hear Ella moving behind him, her soft footfalls on the metal grate telegraphing her exact position.

The window was still up, and so he swung one leg over the sill, then ducked inside. She followed, picking her way gingerly inside, and when he took her hand to help her in, she flashed him a smile. His stomach twisted, and he had to force himself to drop her hand once she was safely inside. All he really wanted to do was enact a scene from his mental movie. But he needed to take care of business first.

He left the window open—it was going to get stuffy in the apartment without the air very soon—and followed her toward the couch. "Where's your stuff?"

"There," she said, pointing to a chest of drawers they'd refinished together their first year in the city. "Bottom drawer is my emergency kit."

He was closer to it than she was, so while she fumbled through the apartment turning off lights and unplugging her computer in anticipation of the power's return, he took the single lit candle from the table and maneuvered to the chest. He opened the bottom drawer and, in the dim orange glow, could see that the drawer was filled with everything they needed. Flashlights, batteries, candles, matches, a tiny portable stereo with a radio and cassette player, even little Sterno cans in case they needed to heat up food.

He pulled the radio out right away, along with a package of size-C batteries. Then he grabbed a couple of flashlights and held them in his hand, weighing the options. The blackout had been unexpected, but he couldn't help but think that it could only benefit him. Flashlights, however, would not.

With one swift movement, he shoved the flashlights under the chest and took only the candles and matches. He shut the drawer, gathered everything up and headed toward the table, still set for dinner.

"Did you find everything?" Ella asked.

"Sure. No problem. You?"

"I got everything unplugged and turned off, and it looks like we've still got water, so that's good."

"Definitely."

He added a few more candles to the table, then placed the rest in strategic places around the apartment—the window, the kitchen, the bathroom—before moving back to join Ella on the small futon sofa. She'd put the radio on the oversize ottoman that doubled as a coffee table and was busy twisting knobs.

"I never listen to the radio," she said. "What news station should I put it on?"

He named the first one that came to mind, but before she could switch the contraption over to AM and turn the knob, he reached out to stop her. "We don't need a news channel. Everyone's going to break programming to talk about this. So we might as well stick with a channel that will have some good music, too. Okay?"

She shrugged. "Sure. But as I said, I never listen to the radio, so…"

"No problem." He took the radio from her, then started twisting the dials, stopping at the station he woke to every morning.

He told Ella as much. "The music's pretty good," he said. "At least, it is when I'm getting dressed." He didn't mention that he also sometimes listened to the station in the evenings and was more than familiar with the program—Sensual Songs and Decadent Dedications. He often thought of her whenever the song selections played. Once or twice he'd even considered calling in a dedication of his own. Usually those were nights when he'd been drinking or had been out on a particularly bad date. Nights when every other woman paled in comparison to El.

Right now, though, the station wasn't broadcasting music. Instead he heard the forced calm in the DJ's voice as he read copy that had undoubtedly been hastily prepared: "…so, it looks like it's a good old-fashioned blackout brought on by the incredible demand for a little air-conditioned relief from the triple-digit heat. Unfortunately the lights are out all over the tri-state area, and authorities are telling us they're not sure when they'll have the power back on. It looks like it's going to be a hot night, so just settle down where you are and stay put. In honor of the blackout, we're going to open the lines for requests and dedications that have to do with hot and summer. And I guess we'll be seeing a bunch of newborns nine months from now. Hey, you've got to pass the time somehow."

Shane turned down the volume and shifted his gaze to Ella. "Looks like we were right."

"That's good to know," Ella said almost distractedly. She was surveying the apartment, her face pulled into a frown.

"What's wrong?"

She shook her head, then pasted on a smile that seemed forced. "Nothing. I was just… Nothing."

On any other day he might push, but tonight wasn't just any other day. He had an approach planned, and pushing wasn't on the agenda. Not yet, anyway.

"It's just such a small apartment," she said after a moment. "And already it's hot in here. And muggy. It'll probably rain, and then this apartment will be like a sauna and we'll be all hot and sweaty and…" She cleared her throat as images of *hot* and *sweaty* filled his mind. He had the overwhelming urge to touch her. Thought he might die, in fact, if he couldn't. And so he shifted, trying to look casual as he trapped his hands under his knees.

Beside him Ella shook her head. "Never mind. Anyway, um, you should stay the night. The subway will be shut down and the streets will be murder. I hope the blackout doesn't screw up your itinerary."

"I'm sure the power will be back on well before Monday," he said, but he spoke the words automatically. His mind was still back on her previous statement—that he was going to stay the night. There'd been something in her voice. Subtle, but he'd been trained to listen to witnesses' voices, to watch their faces. Plus, he knew Ella.

There was something going on there, he just wasn't entirely sure what. Discomfort maybe? Awkwardness? But that couldn't be right. He'd stayed at her place dozens of times—a bit awkward for him lately, particularly when they shared a bed, but never for her. Why would it be? Unless…

He got up and headed to the kitchen, using the motion to hide the flash of hope that he was certain was crossing his face. *Unless his first reaction had been right and that* had *been the heat of desire he'd seen reflected in her eyes.* If she felt that way, then he was already halfway to winning his case. And he didn't even have to stack the jury.

"Hot damn," he whispered, knowing it was past time for him to approach the subject.

"What?"

He jumped, realizing that not only was Ella right behind him but that he'd spoken aloud. *"Hot,"* he said, pointing to the foil-covered pan he'd been reaching for. He held up a finger. "I burned myself."

Even in the candlelight he could see her brow furrow. "Do you want me to find some salve?"

"No, I'm fine." He took a deep breath and took the plunge. Well, not the plunge, really, but he dipped his big toe into the water. "Listen, is there something wrong?"

"Of course not," she said. Her eyes may have widened a bit at the question—it was hard to tell in the dim light—and he couldn't get another look because she turned and started to open some of the containers that were sitting on the counter. "Why? Do I seem like something is wrong?"

He didn't answer right away because he was suddenly tongue-tied, lust overtaking him as she reached up into the cabinets to get their plates. A simple move, and one he'd seen a million times before. Tonight, though, it was as sexy as the dance of the seven veils, the curve of her ass straining against the thin material of her knit pants and practically begging for his touch.

She'd pulled her hair into a ponytail, and a few blond wisps rested on her neck, damp with sweat. He longed to reach out and run a finger down the soft strands. To watch as she shivered under his touch. He longed for that, but he didn't do anything. Not yet. Instead he rested a hip against the counter and tried to sound casual. "You don't seem too keen on my spending the night. Should I head home?"

"Are you insane?" This time she turned back to look at him, her expression reflecting just how idiotic she thought his question was. It was an expression he knew well. When you're friends with someone since second grade, there are a lot of opportunities for them to accuse you of idiocy, and vice versa. "It's a blackout. Every freak in the city will be out trolling. Of course you're not going home."

"Right," he said. "It's just that—"

She waved his words away, then picked up the plates and passed within an inch of him as she headed for the table. "I'm sorry. I'm really glad you're staying. It's your last weekend. I should have invited you to stay the night already. We can sit up and talk and stuff."

The "and stuff" part sounded particularly good to Shane. More, it gave him additional time to implement his plan, letting him ease slowly into it. He hid a grin, thinking about all the witnesses he'd drawn out in long depositions until, by the end, they were putty in his hands. It was stressful but exhilarating.

With Ella there was only exhilaration. Coupled, of course, with a hell of a lot of risk.

But he couldn't worry about the risk. He had to do this, had to put his feelings for her out there and hope that she felt the same. Persuade her to his side if she didn't. One way or another, by the end of tonight, things would be different between them. In the meantime, he intended to do everything in his power to see to it that the difference tilted in his favor.

AS SHANE CLEARED THEIR salad plates, Ella put down the clean flatware, all the while trying to act casual even though her insides were tied up in knots. If she survived this night, it would be a miracle. Already Shane knew that there was something on her mind—why wouldn't he? He certainly knew her well enough.

But knowing that something was up and knowing *what* was up were two different things. And Ella intended to do everything in her power to make sure Shane never became aware of her lapse in good judgment.

Because that's all this was. A tiny little blip in her libido. Nothing permanent and certainly nothing to get worked up about.

Of course, she was now faced with the question of how to keep up the subterfuge. Not an easy proposition, especially considering how fabulous the apartment looked in candlelight and how Shane's green eyes and tanned skin seemed to glow. And—she was a big girl, she could admit it—he looked pretty damn hot, too. And not in an air-conditioner-died sort of way. More like a run-her-fingers-all-over-his-sweat-slicked-chest kind of way.

She could be strong. This was just a libido blip.

She just needed to keep repeating that like a mantra. *Libido blip.*

"You sure you're okay, El? You keep zoning out on me."

"Fine," she said, then smiled brightly. "I'm great." She gestured to the table. "This is just amazing."

"The salad was only to get you warmed up. It's the rest of the meal that will really knock your socks off."

"Just the look of my table's already done that," she admitted. "It looks like I've actually got some style."

Her dingy little table had been transformed. Amazing, since the table hardly qualified as a dining table. It was more like a glorified card table, something that Ella had picked up after her move when she'd realized that all of the furniture she'd cherished in her Houston bedroom would never fit in the tiny hovel that Manhattanites called apartments.

It had been a small sacrifice, though, because in the end she'd found a studio all to herself, which meant she was a rare breed: a student living in the city without a roommate. She liked it that way, though. Liked coming home to an empty apartment and winding down without having to worry about being polite to someone else.

Shane had helped her sell her old pieces and buy the dollhouse-size furniture that now filled her place. Since dollars were tight, they'd raided thrift stores and even schlepped into New Jersey for garage sales.

This table had been one of her favorite finds and it had served her well for years. Usually it was topped with stacks of her books, but tonight, Shane had covered it with a white cloth that, upon a second look, Ella realized was one of her sheets. Atop the sheet he'd put two place settings, cozily arranged across from each other.

If Ella didn't know better, she'd think Shane had been planning to use her apartment to entertain a date.

"Considering all of my dishes are chipped and mismatched, I know this didn't come from my apartment. How did you—"

"No, no, no," he said in a fake French accent, "zee master chef, he never reveals zee secret, no? Zee presentation, she is as important as zee meal, is it not so?"

Ella lifted her brow.

"Come, *ma cherie.* Do not disappoint Chef Shane. You are impressed, *non?*"

"Yes," she admitted, unable to fight her smile. "The table is beautiful. The salad was delicious. I'm totally impressed."

"Then we'll move on to the main course." He placed a hand on her shoulder. "This is a celebration of new cabinets, a going-away dinner for me and an early birthday party for you. I figured we should do it in style."

"No complaints from me," she said, although in her heart she did have one tiny complaint. But she could hardly complain to Shane that he was making it supremely difficult to recover from her recent festival of lust. And then, when he started to rub her shoulders, she just about came undone.

"You're tense," he said.

"Um, yeah. I guess. A little." She started to twist away, tried to casually extricate herself from his touch before the heat generated by his fingers fried her brain.

"Hang on," he said, firmly holding her in place. "What's your hurry?"

"Nothing. No hurry." She was certain she sounded frantic. "I was just going to get up and help you with the food."

"I can handle the food." He spoke softly, his head bent low to her ear so that his breath tickled the back of her neck. Her heart stuttered in her chest, and she was certain her cheeks were flaming red. Thank God for the dim lighting. And thank goodness Shane was standing behind her, where he couldn't get a look at her face. At the moment she was certain that every tiny bit of lust in her body was reflected right there in her eyes.

Slowly his fingers started to knead her shoulders more deeply, and she let out an involuntary moan of ecstasy. "That feels nice," she said, hoping she sounded like a woman with sore muscles and not a woman whose every nerve ending was tingling from the touch of his hands.

"You know," Shane said, "if your course load is making you this tense, maybe you should back off."

"Yeah, right," she said. He knew as well as she did that backing off from her schoolwork wasn't an option. "Besides, that's not what's making me tense."

"No?" he murmured. "What is?"

You. Part of her really wanted to say it, wanted to let him know just how nuts he was making her tonight. Wanted to see what he'd do about it. The other part of her—the rational part—vetoed that plan. "Just everything. You leaving. End of the semester. The heat."

"Hmm."

She twisted to look at him, but his strong grasp prevented her. "What's that supposed to mean?" she demanded. "'Hmm.'"

"Nothing," he said. "Just a noise."

She didn't believe him, but right then it didn't matter. Her body was turning into liquid heat, his hands the catalyst. Her breasts felt heavy, her now-hard nipples pressed enticingly against the soft cotton of her tank top. She closed her eyes and for just a second let herself slide into the fantasy that was pounding in her head. A fantasy involving Shane's skillful hands and her breasts. His palms cupping her, his thumb and forefinger tugging at her nipple until the hot wire that ran from her breasts to her crotch fired, pushing her over the edge into total bliss.

"Do you want more?" Shane asked, and Ella

opened her mouth, lost in a dreamy haze, and almost said *Yes, yes, oh, please, yes.*

She caught herself just in time. "What? More?"

"Champagne," he clarified, and she realized with a start that one of his hands had moved forward to grasp her champagne glass.

"Oh. Right. Sure."

"Good," he said. "You could use a little more. It'll loosen you up a bit."

That was a worry, but she wasn't going to admit that to Shane. And at the moment, getting drunk sounded like a dandy plan. He took his other hand off her shoulder, leaving her both relieved and frustrated, then filled her flute to the brim. She took a sip, forcing herself not to gulp it down and demand more.

He'd drained the bottle filling her glass, and now he moved into the kitchen. When he came back, he was holding a new bottle, the dark bottle slick with condensation.

"Um, Shane?"

He looked up, a question in his eyes as his thumbs gripped the cork. The glow from the candlelight danced in his dark brown hair, and Ella had to force herself not to reach out to see if it was as soft as it looked. She'd touched that hair before, of course, but suddenly it was as if she'd never, ever touched any part of him. Shane Walker was a totally new commodity, and Ella had a sudden premonition that this

Shane was going to keep digging until he discovered her secrets.

"El?"

She realized that she'd never finished her thought. "Oh. I, um, was just going to say that I have to study tomorrow. One bottle is probably enough."

"Sure," he said, but he kept on with that cork. "But if it's all the same to you, I think I might want a little more."

"Oh. Sure. Of course," she said as the cork popped and Shane snagged it soundly with his thumbs.

He topped off his drink from the fresh bottle, then went back in the kitchen to get the rest of the food. Once he'd finished filling their plates, he took his seat across from her. For a moment he just watched her, the candlelight flickering in his eyes. And just as she was starting to squirm under his scrutiny, he lifted his glass for a toast.

"To best friends," he said. Then the corner of his mouth lifted and he looked at her with an intensity that she'd never seen before. "You look really beautiful tonight."

"I—" Her cheeks heated, and she glared at him. "Where did that come from?"

He just shrugged, totally innocent. "I'm just stating a fact. It's no secret that you're pretty. And the candlelight really brings out the gold in your eyes."

"Thanks," she said, but the butterflies that had

settled in her stomach started up again. "You, um, look good, too."

As soon as the words were out of her mouth, she cringed. That was not the kind of thing she should be saying. Not today. Not when he may have picked up on her lust.

Flustered, she took refuge in the meal, suppressing a little moan of ecstasy as the tender morsel practically dissolved on her tongue. "Fabulous," she said.

"I'm glad you like it."

There was nothing special about his tone or the words, but she felt a little shimmy of pleasure nonetheless. He'd done this for her—as her best friend, of course, nothing more—and that was a really nice feeling.

Their already staggered conversation faded to nothing, unable to compete with such amazing food. At some point during the meal Ella realized that her flute—once near empty—was now completely full.

She considered protesting, then decided against it. She'd already decided that a buzz was pretty appealing. And this was a blackout, after all. The normal rules didn't apply.

A little voice repeated that in her head: *the normal rules don't apply.*

She shook her head, ignoring the self-indulgent little voice. That little voice could get her in trouble. That little voice could ruin everything.

They didn't talk much as they finished the meal, though Ella did say how fabulous it was and how surprised she'd been. All true, of course. What she didn't say was how special it made her feel that Shane would go to all that trouble. She thought it, though, and that little morsel of truth sat in her stomach like a rock. Tony had never done anything like this for her. As friends went, Shane really was the best, and she felt a little pang of guilt that while he'd been out preparing this amazing surprise for her, she'd been sitting in a study carrel thinking about his pecs.

They cleared the plates together, the already small kitchenette seeming even more tiny by candlelight. Any residual coolness from the window-unit air conditioner had long since faded, and the air in the apartment seemed thick and heavy, full of the musky scent of Shane, which was driving Ella nuts despite her best effort not to think about it.

As he reached past her to put a dish in the sink, his arm brushed against her shoulder. It was a nothing contact, certainly nothing she would have even noticed before today. Now, though, every nerve ending in her body seemed concentrated on that one spot.

One tiny little haphazard touch. Think of the damage he could wreak if he touched her deliberately with an intent to seduce.

She swallowed, the possibility more than she could bear at the moment, then turned to frown at her stove. She'd reached a hand out without thinking, and now she pulled it back, feeling slightly stupid. "I guess coffee or tea is out of the question. I was just going to heat some water and realized—"

"Kind of limits our options, doesn't it? But we do have dessert, so it would be nice to have something with…"

He trailed off as he turned, his gaze sweeping her apartment before settling on the armoire that served as closet, TV cabinet and, as Shane well knew, wine cellar.

"Got any Frangelico left?"

"Yeah, but it's really only good heated," she said, then cringed. The answer *should* have been, "Yes, but I've had enough alcohol, thanks." Instead she'd left a door wide open.

And Shane walked right through it. "Sterno," he said.

"Excuse me?"

"I saw Sterno cans in your emergency drawer. And I know you have brandy snifters. It shouldn't take long to heat us up two glasses."

"I'm not sure we should—"

"El, it's only a blackout. And from what I could tell, you managed to acquire every Sterno can this side of the East River. Were you planning on cornering the market?"

She grimaced. Maybe she had gone a little over-board, but that didn't mean they could just waste the stuff. "It's still for emergencies, Shane."

"Trust me," he said. "The possibility of drinking room temperature Frangelico qualifies as an emer-gency. Besides, we need something to wash down dessert."

You'd be a nice dessert.

Mortified, she looked away. It had to be the cham-pagne; the bubbles had fizzed her brain. She forced her mind back to mundane things. "Dessert, huh?" she asked as he poured Frangelico into two brandy snifters. "Dare I ask what you got?"

"It's chocolate and dense. That's all I know."

"Really?" Chocolate was her weakness and Shane damn well knew it. "So, um, I get the bigger piece, right?"

"There's only one—" He stopped himself, then continued. "There's only one condition."

"What?"

He smiled, and the way his mouth curved had her feeling a bit damp between the legs. "Never mind. I'll tell you later."

"You're scheming," she said.

"I never scheme. I plan."

"Yeah? Well, I plan to eat some chocolate." She pulled the carton out and carried it to the nearest can-dle. "By the way, what happened to my flashlights?"

"Didn't see any," he said.

"I have about seven of the disposable kind." Considering how much less sensual every little movement would be in the harsh glare of incandescent bulbs, she really wanted to snag them.

He shrugged. "None in the chest."

"I can find them." She started to move across the room but stopped when she saw his expression. "What?"

"Get flashlights if you want, but this is supposed to be a high-class dinner in a high-class restaurant. I think candlelight fits. Don't you?"

"Sure. Of course. I was just—" She shut up. Most likely she was just digging herself in deeper and deeper. "Never mind."

With a single flame to work by, she lifted the lid on the carton and saw one slice of the most amazing-looking chocolate cake she'd ever seen in her life. "Wow," she said. "It looks great, but what are you going to eat?"

He looked up. "What do you mean?"

"There's only one slice. A huge, absolutely delicious-looking chunk of chocolate, but still only one."

He stood up, bringing the Frangelico with him as he moved toward the couch. "Well, it's hardly a crisis." He cocked his head, urging her toward him. "Come on. And bring two forks."

She lifted an eyebrow. "Two forks? I thought the

bigger piece was mine. And this is clearly the bigger piece."

"*Bigger* is a relative term. There has to be something to compare it to. With only one piece, you have to share."

"I don't know, Walker. That sounds like a pretty flimsy attempt to get at my chocolate. I think you'll have to do better."

"Okay," he said slowly. He put the drinks down on the coffee table and rubbed his hands together. "We'll wrestle for it."

"Excuse me?"

"You know. We'll determine who gets the chocolate in the same manner as boxers, martial-arts athletes and superpower nations. We'll fight."

"Superpower nations, huh? I think that means we need to call in the UN."

"I'm a rogue nation, El. I want that chocolate." He was circling her now, his expression playful. She held the chocolate high above her head and turned, her feet dancing as she tried to avoid his grabs.

"Careful," she squealed. "If it falls, neither of us gets it."

"That's a risk you'll have to take. You could just concede and share. That way you're sure to get some chocolate."

"Never," she said. And with that she took off running, moving back around the sofa and ending up with him on one side and her on the other. She'd brought two forks, and now she tossed one on the couch. The other she slipped into the creamy confection and brought a bite to her lips. As Shane watched, she closed her eyes, exhaled and sighed with satisfaction. "Yummy," she said. The word died on her tongue when she opened her eyes. He was staring at her, a hunger reflected in his eyes that didn't seem entirely caused by the dessert.

"Okay," he said, "now you've done it." He climbed onto the futon and made a grab for her. She leaped backward, almost losing the cake but steadying herself before it fell. Too late, though. He was over the couch, his arm catching her around the waist.

She squealed and held the plate high with both hands, then realized what a mistake *that* was, because he pulled her closer. Without her arms for protection, her breasts pressed against his chest. Her nipples hardened and her breathing came in shattered, raspy bursts. Her lips felt full and her whole body flooded with a warmth fueled by need.

And it wasn't a need for chocolate, that was for damn sure.

"Ella?" His voice, low, seemed as soft as a caress. His brow furrowed, concern turning his eyes a deep jade. "Are you okay?"

She spun away, right out of his arms, and brought the plate down in front of her, the cake suddenly a buffer between the two of them. "I'm…of course… yes. I mean, why?"

He cocked his head, studying her, and Ella was absolutely certain he could see every thought in her head. And so help her, she *wanted* him to. Against every ounce of better judgment in her body, she just wanted to jump in and go with the flow and lose herself in—

American Pie.

She blinked, confused, as she realized the tinny melody of Don McLean's "American Pie" was filling the room. "Oh!" She jumped, suddenly remembering. "That's my phone. That's Tony." She'd assigned different rings for different friends, and that was Tony's assigned tune.

Saying a silent thank-you to the patron saint of cell phones, she scurried away from Shane, then dropped to the floor beside the couch. She set down the cake, and when her fingers found her purse, she dug out her phone. "Hello? Tony? Hello? I'm here!"

"Ella?"

"Tony! Hi! I was afraid it would roll over to voice mail. It's so great to hear from you. I miss you." The words were bubbling out of her faster than she usually spoke, and she could only hope that he attributed her excitement to enthusiasm and not the real cause: guilt.

"I miss you, too." His voice seemed to hold a hint of a smile. "It sounds like you're doing okay, then. You're going to be okay tonight?"

"What?" She blinked. "What are you talking about?"

"The blackout. I just saw the news. I was wondering—"

"Oh! Right. I'm fine. And I'm sure they'll get the power back on by morning."

"Hmm." Tony sounded less than confident. "I hate the idea of you going through that by yourself."

"Not a problem. Really. Shane was here. He was—"

"Shane?"

Ella closed her eyes and drew in a breath, renewed guilt—foolish, since she hadn't *done* a thing—flooding through her. "He was here when the power went out. He refinished my kitchen cabinets while I was at the library today. They look great."

"Nice," Tony said. "But I told you we'd do a total remodel later in the summer."

"I know, but…" She trailed off with a shrug. It was so much nicer to have had Shane put in the work than to have Tony whip out his credit card. "It was his idea," she said after a beat. "A going-away present."

"Is he still there? Is he staying the night?"

"No." The lie came automatically to Ella's lips. "Of course not." She turned, giving Shane her back, afraid that he'd be able to read the lie in her expression.

"He left right after the blackout?"

"Right."

"Bastard," Tony muttered.

"Excuse me?"

"Didn't he even think that you might want company? I mean, there's no power. There could be looters. There could be—"

"Tony," she interrupted. "I'm fine. And you need to get back to work, don't you?"

"Yeah, actually I do. I just saw the news and wanted to call."

"Great," she said. Her phone beeped, and she pulled away long enough to check the screen. "My battery's about to die," she said. "And I can't recharge without power, so we should cut this short. I'll see you on Wednesday?"

"Absolutely. Shall I come over straight from the airport?"

She remembered her plan to seduce him in the sexy nightie. But that plan would have to wait since she already had another agenda in place for Wednesday. "Sure. We can catch a taxi from here to SoHo."

A pause, then he asked, "Why are we going to SoHo?"

"I promised Leah we'd go with her to an opening." It sounded like a ton of fun, and Ella loved going out with Tony's sister. "The show's by some artist she's dating and she's totally nervous. Matty's going to be there, too," she added, referring to his second sister. "Maybe even your father."

"A real family affair," he said, but without any of the enthusiasm she felt.

"Well, yeah. But we can come back to my place after." Actually she and Leah had talked about the possibility of Leah, Matty, Ella and their dates renting a helicopter for a nighttime sky tour of the city. From the sound of Tony's voice, though, she didn't think now was the time to pitch it. She'd pick a time when he was more amenable. Like never.

"Well, I suppose we can go, but let's not plan to stay too long. By the way, have you and Leah gotten together since I've been out of town?"

"Checking up on me?" she asked, unable to prevent the edge that crept into her voice. She knew well enough that Tony thought Leah was too much of a party girl. Ella knew better. Leah just liked to have fun. She wasn't reckless or foolhardy. She didn't slack off at her job. She just liked people and she liked dancing and she liked the rush that came from exploring the city. Ella totally empathized. Tony, unfortunately, did not.

"I'm just curious."

"Right," Ella said. She almost picked an argument, but her battery was low and, since they'd had this battle before, she knew the outcome. Stalemate. She'd continue to hang out with Leah and Tony would continue to complain and life would go on as usual. According to Leah, that was simply one aspect of the family's dynamic. Always had been, always would. "But no, since you asked, I haven't gone out with Leah in a few days."

"Good, then." There was a muffled sound while he talked to someone away from the phone, then he said, "Okay, I've got to go. Love you."

"I love you, too," she said, and this time she turned around and flashed Shane a radiant smile, feeling as if in some small way she'd scored a victory. She just wasn't sure what she'd won.

5

"Everything okay in paradise?" Shane asked as she slid her phone back into her purse.

"Oh, sure." She stood back up to find him holding the plate of chocolate cake.

"Hmm."

She lifted an eyebrow, suddenly feeling tense and edgy. "What?" she demanded.

He just stared at her. "I didn't say anything."

"You didn't have to. That little noise you made was enough."

"Dammit, Ella. You're the one dating Tony. Does it really matter what I think?"

She should have said no; she really, really should have. Instead she said, "You're my best friend. Of course I want to know what you think."

"I think it seems like you're fucking the family, not the man."

"What?"

"Come on, Ella. Every time we talk, you're raving about something you did with Tony's family or with his sisters or something funny his dad said. So who are you in love with? The family or the man?"

"I take it back, Walker," she said, bristling. "I don't want to hear your thoughts."

For a moment she thought he was going to argue, but he stayed quiet, then nodded and muttered a soft, "I'm sorry. It's none of my business." He held up the chocolate. "Peace offering?"

"I…" She trailed off, suddenly uncomfortable and desperately afraid that there was more truth in his words than she was willing to admit. "You can have it. I'm fine." She turned around, making a pretense of moving one of the candles away from the wall.

"El? I said I was sorry."

"I know. I'm fine. Really."

"Is there something else? What did Tony have to say?"

"Nothing," she said. "It's nothing at all. I…I just realized how full I am. Truly."

"Well, come over here and sit at least. Don't you want your drink?"

Actually she did want the drink. Would have liked to get good and drunk and pass out in her bed and wake up when this was all over. That probably wasn't an option, but a few sips of liqueur would take the edge off.

She moved around the couch, then took a seat in the far corner. It was a futon couch, the kind where the back folds down into a bed. And it was, in fact, her bed. But she tried not to think about that as she sat there sipping the warm, fragrant drink.

Shane sat at the other end of the couch, but unlike her, he wasn't jammed into the corner. Instead he was casually leaning back, his shoulders seeming incredibly broad against the back of her white sofa. She shifted in her seat, suddenly feeling even more warm, and she eyed the air conditioner with longing.

"It is hot in here," he said, then took a bite of cake, managing to chew and swallow even with a wicked grin.

"Don't choke on it," she said, feeling surly.

He laughed. "Do you remember tenth grade?"

"When we got trapped in the theater and they locked the school—"

"And McCullough killed the lights and we couldn't figure out how to turn them back on." He picked up and finished her thought, and she couldn't help but grin at their easy rhythm.

"This feels kind of like that," she said. "Stuck in the dark with no power."

"In a lot of ways." He shifted, casually draped his arm on the back of the couch, his fingertips not quite touching her shoulder. "I remember thinking it was an adventure and how glad I was that I'd gotten trapped with you."

"You are such a liar!" She tossed a pillow at him.

"I distinctly remember you telling me you wished that Diana Madison was there."

"True," he conceded. "But that was only because I wanted to make out with her. Since the feeling wasn't mutual, I would have ended up spending an entire night talking drivel with her. You, I *wanted* to talk to."

"You thought she talked drivel and you still wanted to get in her pants?"

"Being a gentleman, I'll only admit to wanting to get in her shirt."

"Some gentleman."

He pointed to himself. "Is that a dig I hear? I'll have you know I was a paragon of virtue. I didn't try anything with you, did I?"

"You *never* tried anything with me."

"True. Now why is that?" His fingers slid down and brushed subtly over her shoulder. "I mean, you were hot back then. Not quite as hot as you are now but definitely smoldering."

She swallowed, not sure what to say. What to do. His hand barely touched her, and yet she was certain she had scorch marks along her shoulder from the fire his fingers ignited. Only yesterday his touch would have been a refuge. Now it was a danger zone. "Kind of astounding, huh?" she finally managed. "I mean, both of us being teenagers with raging hormones. And yet we went a whole night in the dark." She licked her lips and drew in a breath. "I guess it was just the same as it's always been. You know. Our friendship is too important to risk screwing up, even back then."

"Especially back then," he said.

"What do you mean?" She cocked her head, trying to read the undercurrents in his statement, and didn't even notice that he'd pulled his fingers away.

"Our lives were such a mess back then. We cleaved to this friendship. We held on tightly to each other and that's what kept us both from drowning."

She nodded. That was true enough. In a lot of ways, they'd raised each other. She'd grown up hating that her family was missing-in-action and desperately wanting a family of her own. Needing it. But that need hadn't ever diminished the importance of what Shane had been—still was—to her.

"It's different now," he said almost as if he'd read her mind. "Now we've managed to get ourselves settled. We have lives and careers that matter to us. We're not teenagers trapped in warring or neglectful families. We're not looking for those kinds of ties anymore."

"Yes, but—" She didn't know what to say. She knew she wanted to argue, because somehow he seemed to be diminishing what they had now. But she didn't quite know *how* to argue.

"Come on," he pressed. "You know I'm right. It's

different now. That night you told me every little detail about you and Chris Tobias. Believe me, I'm not expecting to hear the details about you and Tony tonight."

"I *so* didn't tell you every detail about Chris."

"Did, too."

"Did not."

"What about your tingling toes?"

She squirmed a little. "Everyone thinks about tingly toes."

"Yeah, but you admitted he didn't make your toes tingle. If memory serves, you went into great detail about the way he kissed and how you kept on kissing him hoping that your feet—and the rest of you—would start to tingle."

"Yes, you're right. But I was—what?—sixteen? I wanted grand romance, passionate kisses and tingly toes."

"So what did you do?"

"I broke up with him. You know that. We spent the whole night analyzing how I felt, and the next day I broke up with him."

"Because you deserved to have your feet tingle."

"Exactly."

"And Tony?"

She glared at him. "I'm not on a witness stand here, Shane."

"See? That's exactly my point." He gestured between the two of them. "*Our* relationship has changed. Back then you didn't mind discussing Chris at all. But now you're not inclined to discuss Tony."

"We've discussed Tony."

"A bit," he agreed. "But not the nitty-gritty."

"That's not a change in our relationship. That's because I wasn't in love with Chris. I am in love with Tony."

"So he makes your toes tingle."

"Yes. No." She closed her eyes and slammed her fist into the pillow. "That's hardly a realistic benchmark for a relationship."

"I'll take that as a no."

"Dammit, Shane!"

He shrugged. "Just making conversation."

"Then make it about something else. This subject is now officially closed."

He shrugged. He'd been balancing the dessert plate on his lap and now he picked it up. She watched as he slid the fork through the chocolate, then brought the utensil to his mouth. His lips closed over it and he withdrew the fork, closing his eyes as he did so. El just stared, her earlier irritation forgotten as lust zinged through her body and collected between her thighs, leaving the rest of her feeling hollow, as if she needed something—or someone—to fill it.

"Sure you don't want some?"

"What?"

He held up the plate. "Dessert? Want some?"

"Oh. Um, yeah. Sure. What the hell. I'll take a bite."

His smile was slow and easy. "Great." Before she could protest, he dipped his fork in, then held it out to her. She hesitated for only a second, but that was long enough to provoke a twinkle in his eye and a "Come on, El. I don't have cooties."

She shot him a dirty look, then opened her mouth. The chocolate set her taste buds tingling, and when she realized how close Shane had scooted to pass her that little bite, the rest of her body followed suit.

She closed her eyes, hoping he thought she was simply enjoying the decadent treat. In fact, she was afraid to look at him, afraid he'd see the truth in her eyes.

"Good, isn't it?" His voice was low and right there, and she knew that if she leaned forward, she could capture his mouth with a kiss.

She didn't, of course. Instead she opened her eyes, took a deep breath and nodded. "Very good," she said.

He was looking at her, his expression guarded as if he expected her to say more.

She cleared her throat. "This was really nice. The whole dinner thing, I mean."

"I'm glad you liked it." That mysterious something was still in his voice, and the expression on his face suggested that she was missing something. He had to be wondering what was up with her tonight, and she seemed completely incapable of getting her head back on straight.

It really was a good thing she hadn't moved to New York to be an actress. She would have crashed and burned by now.

He lifted another forkful of wonderfulness to her mouth, and she took it, this time casually, without having to shut her eyes to hide decadent thoughts of Shane. Good. Nice to know she was managing to wrangle a bit of control over her own emotions.

She was sitting there feeling pretty pleased with herself when he dropped the next bomb. "So," Shane said, leaning back casually against the armrest so that he faced her straight on, "I was flipping through the books you had on the table earlier. Pretty hot stuff."

The books she had on the table!

The sense of self-control vanished with a puff. She knew exactly which books he was referring to. Her erotica collection. The books she'd been using to prepare for her class with Ronnie and to write her paper.

"How do you read them and keep your thoughts, you know, academic?"

"Um, what do you mean?"

He shrugged, looking at her in that way that he had, as if he could see right through her. Considering how well they knew each other, he probably could. "I figure it must be difficult to focus on the academic implications when the whole point of the words is to get you primed for…other things. Especially since I know how fascinated you are by the course material."

Heat flooded her cheeks as mortification spread through her body. *Stupid, stupid, stupid.*

Ella wasn't exactly an innocent, but she'd never read erotica before taking the course. And that first week, when she'd started flipping through the pages of an anthology of stories from *The Boudoir,* her fingers had almost caught on fire from the heat generated by those words.

And her fingers hadn't been the only thing to heat up. It had taken her almost an entire Saturday to read the book, primarily because she kept having to take breaks to, well, scratch the itch that the heated words had caused.

That part hadn't been stupid. It had been decadent and fun and even now the memory made her a little hot. What had been stupid was telling Shane back then how she'd reacted to the material. But at the time it hadn't occurred to her that she might feel just as lustful toward him. That fantasies of her best friend could make her even hotter than those carefully crafted words on the page. Or that he'd be sitting in her living room asking her to discuss those words and that she'd have to manage it without revealing how much she wanted *him* to scratch the itch that was starting to tingle so appealingly between her thighs.

"El?"

"Um, sorry. I was just trying to think of how to answer that. I, uh, guess it's a question of academic interest. I mean, I'm steeled for studying, so the words aren't playing with my head because I'm not letting them." Or at least she was trying not to let them. Considering her little fantasy in the library, she wasn't succeeding very well.

She took a sip of her Frangelico and tried to look as if she was still considering the question. "I suppose it's just a question of self-control," she finally said.

"That makes sense." His smile broadened, and he looked so damn sexy that she grabbed a pillow and pulled it up against her just to have something to do other than gawk at him. "You must have a lot of self-control, then. Some of what I was reading put me right over the top."

"You weren't trying to analyze it for a term paper."

"No," he said with a heart-stopping grin, "I wasn't."

He got up and moved around the sofa, coming back with a copy of Nicolas Chorier's *Satyra Sotadica*. "Like this, for example." He opened the book and leaned in close to the candle. "'He tells me to sit down again as I was seated before and places a chair under either foot in such a way that my legs were lifted high in the air and the gate of my garden was wide open to the assaults I was expecting.'" He closed the book, then looked at her with a tiny smile.

"I'll admit the garden-gates bit is a little over-the-top, but overall that's pretty hot imagery."

"Well, yes. Yes, it is." She could tell he wanted her to say more, but her brain wasn't quite working. She'd tried to be academic while he'd read the passage, really she had. But instead all she could think about was *her* sitting like that and Shane reaching out to touch her.

He was still staring, and she knew she had to say something else. "Uh," she said, "yeah, it's definitely charged. Um, that's Chorier for you."

"I just don't know how you do it," he said, all casual and self-assured, his arm resting on the back of the couch. "You or Ronnie, for that matter." He leaned forward just a little, and there was a glimmer of mischief in his eyes. "Jack must be the luckiest man on earth," he added, referring to Ronnie's husband. "Tony, too."

"Get your mind out of the gutter, Walker."

His brows lifted. "The gutter? Tsk-tsk. I don't think what happens between two consenting adults is the gutter."

Neither did she, but since *nothing* remotely related to what she read in the various bits of erotica had happened between her and Tony, she really didn't want to go there.

"I mean, it seems to me that would be a fun way to pass the time in bed. You know, a little reading aloud. Maybe reading to each other." He flashed a lazy smile. "Maybe even acting out a few choice scenes."

Ella swallowed, remembering how she'd fantasized about that very thing just hours before. And not with Tony. With Shane.

"You're right," she said, steeling herself. "Not that Tony's imagination needs any help, but it's kind of fun sometimes to just go with someone else's flow." That was about as bold a lie as she could have concocted, but she figured it would suit her purpose.

From his expression, though, she had to wonder if she was wrong. He looked entirely too dubious. And when he said, "Tony?" in that disbelieving voice, she wondered if she'd gone too far.

She narrowed her eyes. "Yes, Tony. Why? Is that so hard to believe?"

"Yeah," he said. "It is."

She wanted to protest, but she couldn't quite form the words. It *was* hard to believe and she knew it. "Dammit, Shane. So what? So that's not his thing. There's nothing wrong with that."

"Nothing at all," Shane agreed. "So long as you're okay with it."

"Why wouldn't I be? It's not like he's celibate. We have a perfectly fine time, thank you very much." She clenched her fists, realizing she'd spoken out of temper. "Dammit! I didn't want to talk about this. It's none of your business."

"That's just what I'm talking about," he said, his voice soft. "Our friendship is changing, El. Five years ago—hell, even one year ago—you wouldn't have held back."

She closed her eyes. "I'm marrying the guy, Shane. I think I owe him the courtesy of keeping our sex life private."

He nodded. "Yeah, okay. That's fair. But tell me this—is that really the reason? Or are you afraid that if you talk about it—get it out in the open—that it'll kill your fantasy that everything between the two of you is perfect."

"It *is* perfect," she growled. "And it's time we drop this, okay?"

She expected him to argue; the man was a lawyer, after all, and he knew when to push a witness. But he nodded in agreement, and she allowed herself one quiet sigh of relief. If he *had* pushed, she wasn't sure that she could have pushed back. Because the truth was, he was right. Partly, anyway.

Her sex life with Tony wasn't perfect, but everything else about their relationship was. Marriage was about compromise, right? She could live without a wild sex life. She could. After all, she still had her fantasies.

She just needed to work hard to make sure those fantasies weren't about Shane.

6

SCORE ONE FOR TEAM Testosterone.

Shane kept his facial expression bland and had to thank his intensive legal training. He wanted to break into a grin so wide it was painful, but he'd managed not to show a hint of emotion during the depositions of drug-smuggling scum. And he could manage to do the same here.

Phase one, he thought, had gone perfectly.

Just as in a deposition, the first step was to play good cop. Be the witness's friend, get them to trust you, to open up. He felt a little bit of remorse for playing the game with Ella, but not too much. In this case, he thought, the end definitely justified the means. And he needed her thinking about Tony. More, he needed her thinking about the fact that Tony didn't sizzle in the bedroom the way Ella wanted. The way Shane was sure that *she* sizzled.

For a moment there, he'd been a little worried that he was wrong. That he'd looked at Tony and seen the boring, staid guy that he wanted to see and that the man was different with Ella, that he had a wild side, a side that understood Ella's penchant for adventure. But that wasn't the case, as Ella had more or less admitted. It must, he thought, drive Tony crazy that Ella had more in common with his daring sisters than she did with him.

Lord knew it drove Shane crazy. And if she weren't blinded by the bright light of Tony's entire family, Shane firmly believed it would drive Ella crazy, too.

His plan, in a nutshell, was to dim that light so that Ella could see more clearly the faults of the relationship she was in. And hopefully she'd also see that she already had a perfect relationship with Shane just waiting to be raised to the next level.

He glanced over at his briefcase, still sitting on the floor near the kitchen. Time to pull out the papers inside. Time to move on to Phase two.

"I brought some stuff for you," he said.

She squinted at him, clearly not trusting him. Smart girl. "What kind of stuff?"

He held up his hands, a universal indicator of surrender. "Come on, El. Chill out. You said to shift gears. I'm shifting."

"Fine. Okay." She relaxed. A little, anyway. "What kind of stuff?" Same question, but this time it was asked without the tinge of suspicion.

"I was thinking about the paper you're working on."

"*Shane.* I thought you were dropping it."

This time he was the one aiming the sharp glance her direction. "I did. I'm talking about academia, El. Or are you going to prove my first point—that it's hard to separate the two, academia and intimacy?"

She wanted to argue. He could see her struggle, then saw when calm won out. "Fine, fine. Whatever. So tell me what you were thinking about."

"Remember when you said you were considering comparing historical erotica with the modern stuff?"

"Yeah. I'm still thinking about it. The topic's decent, even if it is a little broad. Why?"

He shrugged. "I just thought I'd help you out a bit. On the modern end."

"So…what? You went looking for samples of erotica for me?"

"Found some, too. Had to slog through a lot of stuff, but I remembered some of the historical pieces that you mentioned before and I tried to find ones that tracked. It took a while, but I think I found a couple of good pieces for you." Not entirely true. He hadn't really had the time to research modern erotica. And he'd wanted the particular pieces to be written a certain way. Because, in truth, he wasn't interested in her project, he was interested in his.

So he'd written the pieces himself…with Ella in mind. That had made for an interesting few evenings, that was for sure, and he felt himself get hard yet again as he remembered the fantasies that had accompanied putting the words to paper.

Now she was grinning at him, her eyes dancing mischievously. "Things a bit slow with the law?"

"Just doing my duty for a friend. I'm sure if I needed help, you'd jump in and pick a jury for me."

"Would the jurors be romping around naked?"

"Probably not," he said. "But considering some of the panels I've had to voir dire, I think that having them clothed may be for the best."

"Was there naked romping in what you researched for me?"

"Maybe just a touch." He tried to keep his voice serious, but he was having a hard time of it.

"Hmm. Sounds to me like you got the better end of the helping-a-friend-in-need deal. Well, all right, then. Let's see what you got for me."

He drew in a breath, partly charged, partly nervous. This was it—the line in the sand. *Now,* he thought, *the plan really started.* And he hoped to hell it worked.

ELLA FROWNED AT THE SHEETS of paper he handed her. She'd expected a book, not what looked like straight text, formatted more or less like your typical term paper. "What is this?"

"I, um, found it on the Internet," Shane said with a shrug. "I couldn't get the Web page to print right, so I had my secretary type it up. I figured, you know, if you thought it was helpful, I'd give you the URLs. Later. They're at my office. On my desk. Somewhere."

She had to smile. Shane was never flustered, but he seemed a bit unsettled about this. "Internet porn," she joked. "And getting Sheila involved. My, my. What is the world coming to?"

That seemed to snap him out of it. "One, it's not porn, it's erotica. I believe you're the one who has described the difference to me often enough. And two, Sheila thought it was a hell of a lot more interesting than transcribing my last set of notes with regard to personal jurisdiction and the RICO statutes."

"Okay. Sorry. No more teasing. I know how much you have to do before you move. I really appreciate you taking the time to do some research for me." That was true. What she didn't appreciate was that his actions now had her imagination running overtime. Shane, his tie loosened and his sleeves rolled up as he searched the Internet for erotica. His thoughts drifting to her. His fingers drifting to—

No.

She rubbed her palms over her face. Exhaustion and too much alcohol were a potent mix, especially when she was in close quarters with such a potent man.

"El?"

"I'm fine. Just tired. Getting punchy."

"What better state of mind to read erotica?" he

said, and she could practically hear the smile. "Check out the one on top. It reminded me of that Victorian piece you showed me a few months ago about the artist who seduced his model. Remember?"

She swallowed. Oh, yeah. She remembered. That piece had triggered a particularly vivid fantasy involving a camera and very little clothing. With Tony behind the camera, of course. At least, that's the way she'd played it when she'd described it to Shane.

"So read it and tell me if you think you can work it into your paper."

"Why are you so interested in my term paper?"

"If you'd read the pages of research I've been working on lately, you wouldn't have to ask that question."

"You're the one who wanted to go to law school," she said with a grin. "Of course, if television imitates life, you're having wild liaisons with the paralegals, secretaries and other attorneys in the elevators and in the conference rooms."

"So true," he said. "And now you know the extent of my sacrifice when I took time out to do this research for you." He pointed to the paper. "Read."

She did, and while she did, he came over and poured another glass of Frangelico, heating it over the little container of Sterno.

"Wow," she whispered.

"Read it out loud," he said. When she lifted an eyebrow, he added, "I worked hard for that. I deserve to at least get a little vicarious toe tingle going."

Those butterflies started twisting in her stomach again. This was not the kind of stuff she wanted to read aloud to him. Not today, when he'd been filling her thoughts so completely. On any other day she would have happily read it to him—hell, they would have discussed it in detail and applied it to their own sex lives. So if she wanted to be the Ella he knew, she had to suck it up. Which was, she thought, a particularly poor choice of words.

"He watched me," she read, leaning close to the candle so she could make out the words. She realized that her throat was so tight that her words were barely a whisper, so she cleared her throat and tried again.

"He watched me undress, and though I'd come with the purest of intentions, my body tingled in anticipation. I felt his eyes on me, cool and professional, judging the way the light bounced off my skin, the way the shadows caressed my curves. I reached back and unzipped my dress. The cool air of his studio whispered over my back. I closed my eyes and pretended his hand was touching me there, just above my ass."

Ella swallowed, realizing that *her* back was tingling, primed for a lover's touch. She closed her eyes, drew in a breath and started reading again, focusing on the words of the page so that Shane wouldn't focus on her.

"I reached up, crossing my arms over my breasts to reach the thin straps of the dress. There was no need, I could have easily shrugged the thin material off. But I needed the contact. I was desperate for it. And I used the motion to caress my own breasts, to feel my nipples harden under the flesh of my arms, as the dress fell to the ground.

"He stood there, behind me still, and though I didn't turn around, I knew that he was watching me and that his professional eye now held a hint of heat. I wore nothing except my panties and the black stiletto pumps. I placed my hands over my breasts, a gesture that I hoped he would perceive as modesty. But there was nothing modest about it, and I stifled a groan of pleasure as I pinched and pulled my nipples between my thumb and forefinger, my back still to him."

"What do you think?" Shane asked, taking advantage of Ella's brief pause to catch her breath. His voice was low, or she imagined that it was. In the state she was in, with her own nipples hard and her sex throbbing, she wasn't sure that she was in any position to analyze anyone's vocal tones.

"Um," she finally managed after a false start. "Well, the parallel is amazing. I…I'm sure I can use it in the paper. I'll just, um, set it aside for now and work on it—"

"Don't do that." He sat down next to her and squeezed her knee—something he did all the time, but on most days the contact didn't bring her close to orgasm. She stifled a gasp, realizing she hadn't stifled it as well as she'd thought when he looked at her quizzically. "What's wrong?"

"Nothing. Not a thing."

"Finish it." He nodded back toward the paper, his face relaxed, his eyes bright. "I don't know about you, but I'm getting a kick out of it."

"A kick. Right. Sure." She drew a deep breath, trying to stave off frustration. Why shouldn't he be getting a kick? They'd watched porn together, laughing at the really raunchy stuff. And years ago they'd spent an amusing month or so trying to outdo each other in writing the kinkiest letter to *Penthouse Forum*. They'd never planned to actually send anything in, of course, but they'd cracked each other up. So why wouldn't he want her to keep reading? This was just Shane and Ella having fun. That's all. And no matter how hot she was, no matter how wet she was, no matter how desperately she wanted to slip her hand between her thighs and relieve her need, she would focus on staying sane.

"Right. Finish reading. No problem." She took a sip of her drink and started where she'd left off.

" 'Take off your panties,' he said. 'But leave on the shoes. I'll want you on the chaise by the window, where the light is good.' I nodded and did what I was told. I slipped my hand down to my panties to pull them off, but I didn't do just that. I slipped a finger inside, down into my slick heat and over my clit. I didn't mean to come, but I couldn't help it, and I felt myself gasping, my body trembling from the touch. I knew he saw. I knew he knew. And yet he said nothing.

"Emboldened, I stroked myself one more time, just to get my blood up, and then I shimmied out of my panties. I left them on the floor, then looked over my shoulder to him. He was standing by the camera, a light meter in his hand. His face was bland, professional. But there was desire in his eyes. And I knew. He wanted me. Knowing that, I almost came again."

"I, um, really think that's enough reading aloud," Ella said. She finished off the fresh glass of Frangelico in one gulp, coughing and blinking a little as the strong scent filled her nose and wafted past her eyes. "I've been drinking so much, the words are swimming on the page." It was a good excuse. She hoped he bought it. The truth was, she'd skimmed ahead. The model, her legs spread for him on the chaise. The stream of sunlight dancing on her clit. His camera focused on her. The woman making love to the camera. And then making love to him.

"All right," Shane agreed. "But you like it? For your paper, I mean."

"Oh. Yes. Absolutely. Thank you."

"Anytime." He reached over, casually topped off her glass.

"Oh, Shane. I don't know. I really shouldn't keep drinking."

"Why not?" He passed the glass to her. "So long as we're in a forced blackout, we might as well take advantage of it. What better way to pass the time than to drink and eat?" He paused a second, his eyes never leaving hers, before continuing on. "Of course, I can think of one better way. I guess it's the first time I've regretted us being best friends."

"Excuse me?"

"I just meant under the circumstances. We have a sultry, hot room, pitch-black except for the glow of candles. Fine food. Erotica. A pretty decadent setup, don't you think?"

Alarm bells sang in her head. "Yes. Yes, very. But we *are* friends. And I have a boyfriend. And..." She trailed off, certain the liquor was making her head mushy because she couldn't seem to find another protest. "I can't think about this. My head is starting to throb."

"Turn around."

When she just sat there, he made a circle motion with his fingers.

"Around," he said again.

Warily she complied, and he pressed his fingertips over her temples. She sighed, unable to fight the image of those hands stroking her cheeks, her neck, her breasts. She knew she should pull away, get out from under that fantasy, but his fingers *were* working magic on her head, and it *was* her fantasy. A secret. He didn't know and he didn't have to find out.

She could enjoy his touch, enjoy this fantasy, and be secure in the knowledge that in just two days Shane would be fifteen hundred miles away, his magic fingers no longer any threat.

"Did you ever tell Tony?" he asked.

"What?" Her voice squeaked and she tried again. "Tell him what?"

"About wanting your picture taken. You know, like that."

Her cheeks burned, and for the first time she decided that maybe having a guy friend to share little sexual fantasies with wasn't such a great idea after all.

"I…" She trailed off, remembering the shocked look on Tony's face when she'd suggested he take a few pictures of her. They'd just made love and she'd felt warm and sensuous, and the thought that Tony could capture that through the lens of the camera… well, it had made her hot all over again. Tony, however, had been less than enthusiastic. "We decided that maybe taking pictures wasn't the best idea."

He didn't respond. She couldn't see his face, and it took every ounce of self-control not to turn around and look in his eyes. Ella was certain he was disapproving, being critical of Tony, when Tony had simply been true to himself and his own comfort level. Nothing wrong with that, right?

"Have you ever thought of doing it without Tony?"

"Doing it? Doing what?"

"The pictures, El. I could take them for you."

His hands were no longer on her temples. They'd moved down, now stroking her bare shoulders. He leaned closer from behind, his lips close to her ear and his breath tickling her lobe and driving her crazy.

"You're kidding, right?"

"Not at all. Why should you be denied a fantasy just because your boyfriend doesn't want to share it with you? And we'll do it on the digital camera. If you want to print one out later, you can. Or else you can just keep the files on the computer. Like a little secret only for you."

And for Shane, she thought. And even though she knew that wasn't where he was coming from, in her current mind-set she had to admit that the idea of Shane looking at her from behind the camera was appealing. Erotic, even. He wouldn't be touching her, so it wasn't like cheating. But he'd be watching her, so it would be a little like playing out her fantasy. And so help her, even if that was a really bad idea, she wanted it. If for no other reason than to get it out of her system.

"Come on, El," he whispered. "Let me do this for you. It's not like I've never seen you naked…"

He had, of course, and that one little fact turned the tide for her. She wouldn't be doing anything with Shane they'd never done before. Well, except documenting it with a camera. He *had* seen her naked. He was her best friend. She'd never been shy around him. And if she said no—if she acted shy now— wouldn't he know something was up?

She latched on to the rationalization, moving it to the forefront of her mind and stomping down hard on the truth—that she wanted this more than she ever would have imagined. That she needed it, even. Needed Shane to see her like that. Sensuous. Womanly. *Naked.*

"All right," she whispered. She swallowed, gathering her courage before it faded away. "Yeah. We can do that."

SHANE'S HEART SKIPPED A beat and he tried to keep his hands steady, afraid she'd feel if he trembled with lust. Afraid that if she picked up on the slightest hint of desire from him, she'd close herself off again.

Carefully he rubbed her shoulders. "Good," he said, managing to keep his voice steady. "You have a camera, right?" If she didn't, his fantasy ended right then and there.

"Yeah. In the armoire. Above the TV."

He smiled. How perfect was that. "Great."

"I—I mean, you... You don't think this is weird, do you? Wanting to—"

He cut her off with a firm "Shhh," then pressed his lips to the top of her head. "There's nothing wrong with knowing your own mind, your own fantasies."

She nodded, and he wondered whether it was him or Tony filling her brain. He wanted her thinking of them both, realizing that with Shane she could share, could be herself, but with Tony she had to stifle her desires. But he couldn't point that out to her. He could only lead her there.

He knew he should take his hands off her, should get up and find the camera. He wanted to see her through the lens, wanted it so badly he was already hard. But at the same time he didn't want to break the connection and he had to fight the urge to slide his hands down to cup her breasts. He wanted to stroke and squeeze them, to make her nipples peak and her heart beat faster. He wanted to slide a hand farther down, ease his fingers under the waistband of her pants, then slowly and methodically slip his hand inside and under the soft satin of her panties until his fingers found the damp curls. He wanted to slide his fingers over her sex, then crook his middle finger down, curling it just enough to find her slit and press home inside her. He wanted to hear her moan, wanted to feel the velvety wall of her body close around him.

He wanted all that, but he didn't take any of it. Instead he just squeezed, then pulled his hand away. He put a pillow in his lap and gave her hand a gentle shove. "Put on a silk robe," he said. "You can start in that and we'll go from there."

She nodded, turned to face him for the first time. Even in the dim candlelight he could see the blush on her cheeks. He reached out a finger and, with a grin, brushed the tip of her nose. "I took photography my sophomore year, remember? I'm practically a professional."

"Right." The blush stayed, but a wide smile crossed her face. "I'll just go get ready for my shoot."

While she grabbed a robe and headed into the bathroom, he checked the camera. Fully charged. And like most digital cameras, there was a screen on the back so that he could show her the pictures afterward. Good.

He wanted her to have this experience, then he wanted her to be able to relive it afterward. Whatever it took for her to realize—to really understand—what she could have with him that she didn't have with Tony.

"I feel a little bit like Kate Winslet in *Titanic*," she said, reappearing in front of him in a thin silk robe that hugged every curve. She looked good enough to eat, and the fact that he couldn't take a little nibble frustrated him so much that he had to turn away, ostensibly to fiddle with the camera. "You know," she continued, "that scene where Leo paints her in the nude. I think she paid him a dime for his services."

She sauntered over to him, close enough that he caught a scent of her perfume. She hadn't been wearing it earlier, and the realization that she'd put it on for this little adventure—for him—just about undid him.

"How much should I pay you?" she asked, her voice teasing but edged with sensuality.

"Don't worry," he said, matching her tone. "I'll be sure to send you a bill."

She licked her lips nervously, then looked away, and he had to wonder if maybe he'd crossed the line, stepping too far into her fantasy. He was about to say something stupid and brash, just to remind her that he was just the best-friend-slash-photographer, but she pulled herself together and smiled at him, the edge of daring returning to her eyes.

"So where do you want me?"

That was a loaded question, but he managed to come up with the appropriate answer. "Sofa, I think. Unless you want to pull out the bed."

She shook her head. "Let's just start here. We'll see how it goes."

"Okay. In that case—" He held up a hand, suddenly tuning in to the sound outside. "Wait. It's raining." He could hear the clatter of the rain on the fire escape, the wind sometimes catching the rain and sending it to scatter on the window. "Bring me a few candles."

She did, not asking what he wanted them for, and he had to suppose she knew. It was no secret that Ella loved the rain. In fact, she thought it was erotic, arousing and totally sexy. She had for years, and whenever she'd had a boyfriend who'd shared her passion for staying in bed during the rain, she'd invariably told Shane she was half in love.

They put the candles on the window ledge and then Shane backed off, nodding in approval at the way the dancing flames lit the raindrops, making the entire window sparkle. "There," he said.

"Should I just…" Her teeth played against her lower lip and her fingers toyed with the sash of the robe. "I mean, should I just drop it?"

"Take it off slowly," he said. He lifted the camera, zoomed in until the image was well framed. "Take it off for the camera."

PART OF HER WANTED TO TIE the sash tight and race across the apartment to the bathroom. But that part of her had been soundly pounded into submission by the rest of her. By an Ella that wanted this experience, wanted to stand naked in front of a camera and know that her image, her body, was being captured forever.

And the fact that it was Shane behind the camera…well, she wanted to tell herself that it didn't matter. That he was simply a person like any other. Someone who could operate the camera. But that was a lie. She was glad it was Shane. She liked the idea of him seeing her, of him framing the shot, considering the lighting. Letting the lens caress her body. Capturing her, naked, for posterity.

She supposed she should be upset or sad or troubled that it wasn't Tony, but she wasn't. Tony didn't understand and he certainly wouldn't approve. That was okay. There was no rule that said you had to mesh with your fiancé on every little detail. And in this situation…where she wanted to lose herself in the experience…well, yeah, she was glad it was Shane.

"Beautiful," he whispered, and she realized that she'd leaned against the side of the window, the candlelit rain behind her, the robe falling off her shoulder so that one breast was exposed. Exposed for him.

A low pressure started between her legs, a telltale dampness that she wanted to stroke. And the more she thought about how much she didn't want Shane to realize, the wetter she got.

Her breathing was shallow, and she closed her eyes, lost only to the sound of the rain and the clicking of the camera. He'd turned off the flash, and she knew that she was illuminated only by the many candle flames. A dim reddish-orange, the color of heat. Of lust.

Her exposed nipple was hard, the areola puckered tight around it. She imagined Shane dropping the camera and coming to her, taking her breast in his mouth. Slipping his hand between her thighs.

She made a little gasping noise, then let the robe fall to her waist, trying to camouflage the sound. He made a noise of approval, and she heard the constant whir of the camera. She opened her eyes, just barely, and saw him through the shadow of her lashes. He was moving a few feet in front of her, shifting and adjusting for the best angle, the best light.

She wanted him inside her.

The thought slammed into her head with a force that startled her. She tried to shove it away, but the more she tried, the more the image of her and Shane, lost to their passion for each other, filled her mind.

It's just the situation, El. That's all. Don't go crazy. Don't do anything stupid.

"Touch yourself, El," he said, and she about cried out with desperation. She didn't want her touch, she wanted his. But the thought of arguing, of *not* touching herself while he watched, never even occurred to her. She slid her hands down between her thighs and stroked herself, her fingers immediately slick with wet heat.

"Come for the camera, El," he urged. "Let me show you what you look like when you come."

"I—I…" She trailed off. There was no point in protesting, not when she wasn't about to stop. The robe fell off, pooling around her feet. She leaned back, her shoulders and back on the bare wall. Her hips were forward, moving in an erotic rhythm as she found her own center, teasing and stroking there, *right there,* as the pressure built and built and built until finally she rocketed over the edge.

And so help her, the thought that it was Shane watching her come sent her spiraling faster and higher.

Her body trembled, and she slid down the wall, her eyes closed as she willed her body back to normal.

"Oh, God, Ella."

Shane. And there she was, naked on the floor.

The haze of her orgasm vanished in a poof, and she scooped up her robe, covering herself despite being about a hundred miles away from any semblance of modesty. She stood, struggling into the robe as she turned away from him. "Shane. I didn't. I shouldn't have—"

"Hush. Shhh." He was on his knees, right beside her, his nimble fingers taking the sash from her shaking hands and tying the sash at her waist. "That was beautiful. The pictures are amazing. And you're amazing for having the courage to live out a fantasy."

She wasn't so sure, but since that was exactly what she needed to hear, she turned enough to look at him. "Yeah?"

"Yeah. Absolutely." He kissed the tip of her nose. "I'm proud of you, El. And I've just got to say, I think I've got the sexiest best friend in all of Manhattan. Maybe even all of the world."

IT WAS THE RIGHT THING TO say, Shane thought, because the haunted, mortified look vanished from her eyes. It wasn't what he'd *wanted* to say. He'd wanted to use very explicit words to get her into bed. He was harder than he could ever remember being, and the idea of not thrusting himself inside her, of not cupping her breasts in his hands and looking into her eyes as he made her come again—well, it was almost unbearable.

But that wasn't what Ella needed right now. She was primed, he could tell that, and he knew he'd had his first victory. If he wanted to win the war, though, he had to move with caution.

Gently he took her hand and eased her to the sofa. He settled her beside him, close, so they could both look at the camera at the same time. He scrolled through the images, each one that passed reminding him of how aroused he'd been watching her make love to the camera. Because that's what she'd done. And he'd about lost it simply witnessing the way the light had caught the curve of her breast. When he'd seen her nipples peak, when he'd caught the expression of bliss on her face, he'd known he had to urge her over the edge.

He hadn't been sure what to expect when he'd told her to stroke herself. Objection, probably. What he'd gotten was a fantasy come true, and it had taken every bit of willpower in his body not to come right there, with the camera clicking away.

"Oh, wow," she said. She looked both fascinated and appalled by the photos. "I can't believe I...you know...did that."

"You needed it. I can't believe Tony doesn't want to see you like this. These photos...you're absolutely stunning."

"He wouldn't get it."

"Maybe you should show him."

She shook her head. "No. No way. He's not..." She trailed off, twirling her hand as she tried to find the words.

"He's not what?" Shane prompted.

"I'm not sure," she said. "I guess he's just not you."

7

ELLA REGRETTED THE WORDS, but they were true. Tony and Shane were so different. And tonight, at least, Shane was everything she wanted.

Long-term, though…

No. She wasn't going to go there. And that meant she couldn't go for the short term, either, no matter how tempting it might be to lean closer, to shift just a little, to rub up against Shane and see if maybe—just maybe—he rubbed back.

"I don't know, El. Are you sure…"

"What?" she demanded when he didn't finish the question.

"I just wonder about Tony. I know you, El. And I don't want to see you living half a life." He nodded to the camera. "You're alive in those photos. Does that mean you're not alive with Tony?"

"Of course not! That's totally absurd. My relationship with him is just different."

"Less sexual."

"It's *very* sexual, thank you very much. It's just…

different." That sounded lame even to her ears, but how could she explain the big picture to Shane? More importantly, why should she have to?

Flustered, she tied the robe tighter, then scooted to the far side of the couch. For an extra buffer—just in case her hands might rebel and reach out to stroke him—she grabbed a pillow and clutched it tightly in her lap with both hands.

"If you say so," he said. "It's your relationship. You're the one it has to work for."

"Exactly," she said. She shifted again, trying to get comfortable and failing miserably. The room was just so damn hot. Even muggier now, with the rain.

Except it wasn't the heat in the apartment that was making her all itchy and uncomfortable and desperate to shed the robe again. No, it was the heat inside her. She had a pilot light nestled right there between her legs, and Shane had come along and fired the furnace. And no matter how much she tried to cool down, she couldn't seem to turn off the lust.

"I can see some guys not wanting to take pictures," he said. "I mean, everyone has a line they won't cross. But I just wonder if your lines are too far apart."

"They're not," she said.

"Good." He got up then and moved into the kitchen.

"What are you doing?"

"Just looking for something else I ran across when I was doing that erotica research for you."

"Oh." She frowned, not sure if she could stand another assault on her senses. "I really don't want to talk about school right now. Maybe we should just, you know, play cards or something."

"It's not school, El," he said. "It's erotica."

She knew she should put the brakes on, but somehow the words just didn't come, not even when he came back holding one of her books.

"Here it is," he said. Then, before she could even open her mouth to protest, he started to read a passage from Harris's *My Life and Loves,* in which the hero finger-fucks a young lady while the two were supposed to be listening to the church organist.

Ella's cheeks heated, her mind putting her in the role of the young woman, with Shane's fingers inside her. Oh, my…

"What do you think?" he asked. "Is that something you'd like?"

Oh, yes…

She blinked, anchoring herself firmly back in reality. "What? Shane, what are you talking about?"

"I ran across it before you got here. I was thinking about what you told me, about how erotica turns you on. And I was wondering if it had the same effect on Tony."

Ella pressed her legs together and hoped he

couldn't see the way her hips were shifting on the sofa. "I don't believe I've ever discussed that particular passage with him." What had gotten into Shane? He'd looked after her all their lives, but this policing of her sex life was just a bit much. She wanted to tell him, but he was already riffling the pages. And, dammit all, she was actually curious as to what he was going to read to her next.

You're a slut, El. A mental slut, fantasizing about your best friend and getting off on him reading erotica while he nitpicks at the details of your relationship with another man.

Oh, yeah. She was in trouble.

"I take it that's a no." He made a little noise, something of a mix between surprise and disapproval. "Interesting. Well, there was another passage I thought might appeal to you. Hang on."

As she gaped at him, feeling a bit like a very turned-on lab rat, he started flipping through the book again. Shadows danced on the ceiling as he moved the candle, reading by the soft orange glow. His eyes seemed deeper and more intense, his mouth more generous. And that one unruly lock of hair made her fingers itch to stroke it. Hell, to stroke him.

A warm languor spread through her entire body, and she knew if she wasn't very, very careful, she'd do something incredibly stupid. Something that would be amazing and wonderful and incredibly satisfying...but also incredibly stupid.

Be strong, Ella.

Determined, she fisted her hands at her sides, telling herself they were just talking. He was just doing the best-friend thing. Making sure she was happily in love. Nothing sensual about that. Nothing dangerous.

She told herself that, but somehow she didn't feel any safer. Especially not with Shane busily thumbing through her books.

She told herself she just needed to make it through tonight. Tomorrow he'd go back to his apartment. And even though they'd see each other before he left, the spell would be broken. And then he'd be in Texas, a safe fifteen hundred miles away. She'd marry Tony and Shane would start dating someone and then her condition would clear up.

Except...

Except the idea that some other woman was going to get a taste of her Shane didn't make her happy. Instead it made her positively miserable.

Damn the man for being so good-looking. And damn herself for having such a vivid imagination.

She just needed to keep reminding herself why it would be a terrible idea to get involved with Shane. And it *would* be bad. She'd risk losing everything. His friendship most of all, but also her relationship with Tony's family, the only real family she'd ever known and exactly the kind of family she'd always wanted. Large and boisterous and interfering and supportive. And Tony himself, too, of course. She'd risk losing him.

And she wasn't willing to risk any of that.

Right. Just stay calm. Toe the line. All that jazz. Maybe even have a few more drinks. With any luck, she'd fall asleep and not wake up until the power was back on. All in all, that would probably be the safest way to approach the situation.

Not that she could fall asleep with him in the kitchen perusing the pages of her books. Pages filled with enough heat and lust to rival what she was feeling.

The flipping of pages became slower, and every once in a while he made a little noise, like a cross between pleasure and surprise.

And with each little flip of the page, Ella's pulse increased, the blood pounding through her veins.

Flip.

She felt light-headed.

Flip.

Bordering on desperate.

Flip.

Enough already! "Dammit, Shane. What are you doing?" Her voice was pitched higher than she wanted, but she congratulated herself on sounding annoyed instead of horny. And as he turned to her, waving the book with an expression of unadulterated fascination on his face, Ella once again wondered how in the hell she was going to survive the night.

"Sorry. I got distracted looking for the passage I wanted to show you. But here it is. Want to hear?"

No, no, no. Common sense begged her to decline. Her mouth betrayed her, though, with a casual, "Sure."

His voice was low, the words sultry and full of promise, as he read two passages from Anaïs Nin. The first was from the point of view of a man making love to a woman, unaware that he was being watched. The other was from the perspective of a man watching a couple make love. The words flowed, making Ella shiver. But it wasn't the images the words conjured so much as the sound of Shane's rich, deep voice, teasing and enticing her.

"What do you think?" he asked. "Intriguing?"

Ella licked her lips. "The passage is hot, no question about that, but why did you want to read it to me?"

"I remembered what you said that time. About the park."

"The park?" She genuinely had no idea what he was talking about.

"Yeah, don't you remember? About a week after I got my new apartment? And we were walking Bruno down by the river and we saw that couple and—"

"Oh!" The memory slammed up against her. They'd been taking a walk, talking about nothing in particular, and suddenly Ella had noticed a couple making out near a stand of trees. It was late and the area was secluded—in retrospect not the smartest place to go for a walk—but anyway, the couple had been making out, hot and heavy, in *public*.

They'd laughed about it at first, averting their eyes as they half ran out of the park and back to Ella's apartment. But later that night when they were playing Truth or Dare—a favorite pastime since grade school—Ella had admitted that she'd felt a little frisson of excitement. Decadent, maybe, but the idea of making out—or even making love—out in the open where anyone could see…

Even now she shivered. Somehow seeing that couple in the park had sparked a fantasy she'd never quite been able to get over.

"So have you and Tony ever…?"

Ella swallowed, then changed the subject. "Is Bruno going to be okay?"

Shane cocked his head, his brows raised. "He's fine. Danny promised to walk him since I was having dinner with you," he added, referring to Shane's neighbor across the hall. "And he's got plenty of food and water. Besides, Danny will probably realize I can't get back and keep the mutt company. You, however…" He trailed off, a hint of warning in his voice.

"What?"

"You're avoiding my question."

"No, I'm not." She considered telling Shane it was none of his business. The trouble was, if their past conversations were any indication, it was totally his business. For that matter, she'd just gotten herself off while her best friend watched. Hardly the time to be prudish about their conversations about her sex life.

They'd always been open about sex. That was one of the great things about having a guy for a best friend—she got the other team's perspective.

Tonight, though, she wasn't keen on sharing. She felt too open, too exposed. And way, way too needy.

But she also wasn't keen on explaining why she was feeling so closemouthed. So instead of explaining anything at all, she simply parried. "Have you?"

"Never," he said. "But I think I may have to rectify that oversight. It seems too delicious to pass up."

She swallowed. She sure couldn't argue with that.

"So aren't you going to tell me?"

"What?"

"You and Tony. I mean, I know *you'd* like it. Doesn't Tony—"

"Shane!"

"What?" He shrugged innocently, then reached for the half-full champagne bottle that had been sitting in ice for the past few hours. He poured himself another glass, then filled her empty flute. "You and I talk about this stuff over a stupid game like Truth or Dare. I figure you and Tony have covered all the bases during real conversations. Right? I mean, you probably *have* stood out on that very fire escape, lights off, bodies all hot and sweaty, just a little tipsy from a nice bottle of wine…."

Ella shifted, more uncomfortable under the persistent rat-a-tat of his interrogation than she wanted to be. "Shane, come on."

"Come on, what?"

"Quit playing games with me." She tried to speak lightly, but it was hard to keep her voice under control, especially since she was picturing in her head exactly what he was describing. Only the man on the fire escape with her wasn't Tony. It was Shane. And it wasn't just any night in particular. It was right now. This moment. This dark, candlelit night that seemed tailor-made for fantasies come true.

"Let's just do that," he said, his voice a whisper.

"The fire escape?" She couldn't help it. The words were out before she could call them back.

He looked at her for a single moment too long, his green eyes deep with questions. Then he shook his head, that smile putting in yet another appearance. "It's an option," he said in a teasing tone. "But I was talking about playing games."

"Oh." She took a deep breath, both disappointed and relieved that he hadn't jumped all over her stupid, stupid half suggestion that he take her out on the fire escape and—

Never mind.

Another breath, and she more or less had her wits about her. She made a show of rubbing her temples. "Sorry. I'm feeling all fuzzy. All these drinks have gone to my head. Games, you were saying. You want us to play a game?"

"Sure," he said. "Why not? It looks like the power's going to be out for a while. And I'm too wired to go to sleep. How about you?"

"I'm wired, too," she admitted. She couldn't look him in the eye, though. She was too afraid he'd see the truth there. Disappointment that he hadn't pressed her. And the absolute certainty that if he'd asked, she would have climbed out on the balcony with him in a heartbeat.

It was definitely a good thing that he hadn't asked.

She pulled herself together and looked at him. "What kind of game did you have in mind? I've got chess, Clue, backgammon, playing cards."

"I was thinking more along the lines of an old standby. You know, a bit of nostalgia before I head back to Texas." He caught her eye, and she knew even before he spoke what he was going to say. "Truth or Dare, Ella. I think we ought to play a game of Truth or Dare."

8

HE WAS TAKING A RISK, no doubt about that. But at this point Shane knew he didn't have any choice. He also had a feeling that the odds were on his side. He'd seen the spark in her eyes and he was absolutely, one hundred percent sure that she was as interested in him as he was in her. The question was whether she'd ever admit it. A tough question with Tony waiting in the wings.

He supposed he should feel guilty about trying to romance—no, *seduce*—Ella away from her boyfriend. But the remorse wouldn't come. Tony was an okay man, but he wasn't for Ella. Shane was. And as the man said, all's fair in love and war. Tonight Shane was waging a little of both.

Ella was tucked up into the corner of the couch, her arms wrapped around her knees. She hadn't answered his question, and he wondered if she thought he'd been joking. He hadn't, of course. Nothing about tonight—about Ella—was a joke to him. And by the time he caught that plane home, he intended to make sure she understood that.

"Well?" he asked, conjuring a teasing smile. "How about it?"

"Truth or Dare?" she asked. "You were serious?"

"I figure it's either that or pop in a movie. But unless you have a battery-powered television and DVD player, I'm thinking that's not an option."

The corner of her mouth twitched. "I do have one of those portable players, actually. Remember? My mother gave it to me last January. It was the supercool high-tech present that was supposed to make up for her being a crappy mom and forgetting to even call me over the holidays."

"Right," he said, mentally cringing. The last thing he wanted to do was invite Ella's mother into the conversation. "I'd forgotten." He cocked his head toward her entertainment armoire. "So what shall we watch? *Holy Grail? Star Wars?" 9 1/2 Weeks?* Okay, so he couldn't manage to say the last one out loud. So much for his take-no-prisoners strategy.

Coward.

Maybe so. But not for long. And if she wanted to start with a movie, well, he could do that, too. A lot of dates started with dinner and a movie, after all. "El?"

"Um, we can't watch anything at all."

"No?"

"The thing hasn't been charged since the winter.

I used it once, then shoved it in the closet with the rest of the crap my mom sends me." She relaxed a little then, looking him straight in the eye with one of her patented Ella Davenport smiles. "You want it? You could watch flicks on your way to Texas."

His heart twisted a little, a reaction to the cavalier note in her voice. He was leaving and it sure as hell sounded as if she'd already made her peace with that. "Sure," he said with a shrug. "Thanks. But we've gotten off topic again. If we're not watching a movie, then…"

"I guess we're playing Truth or Dare." Her arms went back around her knees, her entire posture vulnerable.

Shane didn't want her uncomfortable, but he did want her. He pounced. "Something wrong?"

"What?" She peered at him, baffled.

He gestured, the motion of his hand indicating her posture. "Considering the way you're hiding in that corner, I might as well have asked if you wanted an appendectomy without anesthesia. Is something bugging you? You're not uncomfortable about earlier, are you?"

"I…no. Of course not." She shifted again, this time sitting more casually on the sofa. There was still a stiffness to her body, but Shane figured she'd loosen up. Or, rather, he was determined to loosen her up. "So, um, Truth or Dare, then?"

"It'll pass the time," he said. "Unless you want to just head on to bed."

"What?"

Shane hid a smile and tried to look innocent. Oh yeah. He was certain now. He'd spent the night too many times for her to read anything into his comment other than simply going to sleep. Unless, of course, her ideas about what it meant to go to bed with him had evolved.

"Sleep," he said. "I'm still too wired to go to sleep. But since we don't have power, if you want—"

"Right," she said. "No. I'm not tired either. I mean, awake is fine. The game is fine."

"I figured. Old time's sake and all that." He shifted on the sofa, moving infinitesimally closer as he did so. "When did we first play this game, anyway?"

"High school," she said.

"That much I remember."

"With Joan and Preston and the Tyler twins. At Jimmy Anderson's graduation party."

He nodded, savoring the memory. A group of freshmen—himself and Ella included—had crashed the party. A ballsy, totally nonfreshman thing to do. Exactly the kind of thing he and Ella had done back then. At the time he'd thought she was his coolest friend. Now he was just all the more convinced that they'd been soul mates from the get-go.

"So let's start," he said, settling back against the hard-stuffed pillows of the sofa. "Truth or dare?"

She shifted, a half dozen unreadable expressions dancing over her face. She took a deep breath even as he held his. "Truth," she finally said. "Yeah. Truth."

He nodded, his expression serious. "And so it begins."

She rolled her eyes and whacked him with the pillow before clutching it to her once again, this time looking way more relaxed. "Just ask your question, Walker."

"Do you want more champagne?"

She stared at him. "*That's* your question?"

"Yup. Why? What do you think I should ask?"

She held her hands up, a classic gesture of surrender. "No, no. If that's your choice, far be it from me to belittle it."

"Trust me. I play a take-no-prisoners game of Truth or Dare. There are no softball questions."

"Hmm. Well, I'm still sticking with truth, and the answer is yes. I want more champagne."

He reached over, grabbed the bottle and topped up her flute. "Your turn."

"Oh. Well, that was easy."

He cracked his knuckles. "I'm just easing into it."

Her smile, wide and genuine without a hint of hesitation or nerves, warmed him. He wanted that smile all the time. Most of all, he wanted to see that smile when her head was resting on a pillow and her body was naked under the sheets. Soon. Very soon.

She nibbled on the tip of her forefinger, then nodded. "Okay. Truth or dare?"

"Dare," he said.

"Oh." She frowned, looking slightly flummoxed. "What?"

"I was expecting you to say truth. Give me a sec to think up a dare."

He tapped his fingers.

She glared.

"Ella…?"

"Just hang on. You can't rush perfection." The finger slipped back to her lips, and she ran the pad over her plump lower lip in a way that he found utterly provocative. Ella, of course, probably had no idea that she'd even lifted her finger to her lips, much less that she looked totally sexy doing it.

She pondered for a few moments, then nodded. "I dare you to do a striptease."

"A what?" He wasn't sure what he'd expected Ella to suggest, but that hadn't been among the list.

"A dance. You know. Boom-chicka boom-chicka boom-boom-boom. A striptease."

"Right here? For you?" Okay, maybe this wasn't such a bad dare, after all.

She rolled her eyes. "Hardly. Out there." She

raised her arm, pointing toward the fire escape. "Since you couldn't find the flashlights, we'll have to put candles around you. It doesn't exactly make us even, but it'll come close to balancing the score." A sly grin eased over her face, and her eyes twinkled. Shane's heart did a little flip; he loved it when she laughed. "And I figure I'm one-upping you a little. I mean, you'll have an audience."

"I will?"

"Sure. Blackout. Boring night. The rain's stopped. I figure there's a minimum of at least twenty bored folks in other apartments looking out in this general direction. Maybe if you're lucky, one of the girls will be so impressed she'll track you down."

"I can only hope," he said, his voice dry.

"So you'll do it?"

"Why not?" But he wasn't going to be dancing for the neighbors. This was all about Ella. And he intended to make sure she realized that.

He met her eyes. "You're sure? This is the dare you want me to do?" Even if she didn't realize how hot he was for her, she had to know she'd just taken this game in a dangerous direction. Make him do a striptease, and he might just make her…well, he'd think of something to take the dares up a notch.

She blinked, and for just an instant he saw a hint of realization flash through her features. But then she nodded, one eyebrow rising ever so slightly. "You're not getting out of this one, Walker. Striptease. On the balcony. No holds barred. And you can get your tush out there right now."

SURPRISINGLY ENOUGH, HE DID. Her knees grew weak and her nipples peaked at the idea of watching Shane perform a striptease for her.

Good Lord, had she really thought that? She'd meant perform a striptease for the *neighbors*. Not for her. Never for her.

She crossed her arms over her chest as she followed him to the balcony, determined to make her body come off this tight wire.

He had one leg slung over the window—a position that gave her quite a nice view of his jeans pulling tight against his thigh and ass—when he stopped, then turned back to her. "Don't forget my music. And some candles. The lighting at this venue is atrocious."

She fought a giggle but turned to get the stuff, tossing one comment back over her shoulder. "I think you're enjoying this a little too much. Dares aren't supposed to be easy."

"You should've picked something harder then. I mean, why shouldn't I enjoy it? A dark night and the chance to dance for such a captive audience."

She laughed. "Hardly captive. I can always go back inside."

"You?" He looked at her, his eyes entirely guileless but a smile tugging at his mouth. "I didn't realize you were my target audience. I was talking about your neighbors."

Oops.

"Right. Whatever. I'll get the candles."

She headed back inside, happy for an excuse to get away and force the blood to rush away from her cheeks. Still, she had to admit she was looking forward to the performance, even if she wouldn't ever admit it out loud.

She gathered up a dozen taper candles and tucked them under one arm, then grabbed the radio with her free hand. When she turned it on, "Killing Me Softly" drifted out of the speakers, and Ella grimaced as she put the contraption down. "I thought these songs were supposed to be decadent and sexy."

"Slow dancing," Shane said without missing a beat. "Trust me. This song has some serious potential."

"You know this from experience?" She almost didn't want to hear the answer. Already a treacherous little knot of jealousy had formed in her stomach.

"No, but I'm working with what I've got." He lifted his brows and opened his arms. "We could test the theory. Come on, slow dance with me. Right here. Right now."

She tossed a candle at him. "You're not getting out of your dare that easy, bucko."

"It was worth a shot." He lifted the candle. "If you want me to light this, pass me some matches."

She did, and they went about lighting the candles, dripping hot wax onto the railing, then setting the candles in the warm puddles, waiting for the white wax to harden and hold the tapers in place. Once all twelve were securely set, Ella went around and lit each one, transforming the balcony into a sparkling wonderland.

The song died away, replaced by the DJ's soft voice announcing the next tune: "I'm Too Sexy."

"Now *that* is one you can strip to," she said. "It's fate. Shall I shout out your cell phone number at the end of the performance in case there are any agents or managers out there?"

"Just watch, Davenport," he said. "And prepare to be awed."

She nodded, trying to look serious, but at the same time she wanted to burst out laughing. Nervous laughter, though, because no matter how she sliced it, she was looking forward to this. A lot.

The music cranked up and the lead singer for Right Said Fred started belting out his tune. In front of her Shane swayed and gyrated, more or less keeping with the rhythm of the song. The tune lacked the boom-chicka-chicka tune of a traditional striptease, but the lyrics made up for it, and as the singer stressed how sexy he was, Shane ran his hands over his own chest, his pelvis thrust forward, his fingers working at the buttons of his shirt.

When the singer hit the word *shirt,* off it went.

Dear Lord almighty. The man might be her best friend, but he was fine. Fine, fine, fine. His body all the more amazing in the flickering light.

She should probably tell him. After all, friends complimented each other. She'd keep the rest of it to herself, though. Like the part about how she wanted to splay her fingers over that bare chest, and let her palms tease the smattering of hair there. And the part about how she'd like to press her mouth to his pec and flick the end of her tongue over his nipple, then trail kisses down until she got to his waistband and the fly of his jeans.

His jeans. His hands were there now. His thumbs hooked under the waistband as his fingers slid toward the fly. He was facing her, his eyes closed as he moved to the music. He opened them then, and she saw something dark and hot reflected there.

She swallowed, determined to keep her cool.

"You're supposed to be dancing for the neighbors," she said, her voice coming out in little more than a croak.

"Right," he whispered. He turned, managing to ease out of his jeans as he did so, so that now she had an absolutely stunning view of his backside. He was wearing black briefs, and the candlelight illuminated his skin, accentuating the shadows and making his already hard body look even more delicious.

He'd already taken off his shoes and socks before they'd started playing the game, and now he was down to only that one small piece of cotton. She wanted to reach out and touch his ass. She wanted to press up against him and dance with him. She didn't want him to be her friend anymore. Right then she just wanted him to kiss her, hard and deep, and make her as naked as he was. She wanted—

Stop!

She needed to get a hold of herself. She was almost engaged. She was happy. She wasn't going to ruin everything just because she lusted after some guy, especially not some guy who was her best friend.

The music still blared, and Shane turned slightly. And when he did, Ella's entire world shattered. She couldn't see everything, but she could see enough. The long, hard bulge of his erection.

Dammit all, what had she done?

His hands eased under the waistband of his briefs, and she held her breath, part of her praying that he took them off and Tony be damned, and the other part frantically hoping that he stopped before this got out of control. She might not have been certain before, but she was now. Something was going on here. A chemistry. An attraction. Something between her and Shane.

So what was she going to do about it?

In front of her he turned, his eyes meeting hers, his emerald irises glinting seductively in the glow of candles. He inched the briefs down, and she saw the slightest hint of pubic hair, when the song stopped—and so did Shane.

A second ticked by, then another. He seemed frozen, and she also didn't move.

"Your call," he finally said, his voice a low whisper. "Want me to finish the show?"

The DJ was talking now, rattling on about the cause of the blackout.

Ella shook her head. "No. The…the song's over. You, um, were great."

He held her gaze for a moment, then nodded and reached to grab his shirt from the metal railing. Tension filled the air, and Ella wanted nothing more than to scream, *I lied. Take it all off. Take ME.* She didn't, of course. How could she?

So instead she just stood there and stared as he got dressed. He pulled each piece of his clothes on slowly, and as the clothing covered his body, she felt her senses return to normal. Just lust. Nothing that couldn't be repaired. Or ignored.

By the time he was dressed and the candles blown out, she felt almost human again. And certainly in control. Next time, though, she'd pick a safer dare. Like bungee jumping from the Empire State Building.

"Think anyone liked the show?" Shane asked.

"I did," she said, the words out of her mouth before she could stop them.

"I'm glad. But I meant—"

"Encore! Encore!" The words floated across the alley, slightly slurred, as if the female who shouted them had been drinking.

Ella looked at Shane, who looked right back at her. And then they both burst into peals of laughter and clambered through the window. They fell in a heap on the rug, still laughing. "Someone did," Ella said. "Oh, Shane, I think you've got a hot date if you want it!"

That set them off again, and they laughed some more until they both were exhausted. They lay there, Shane's head on Ella's thigh, a position they'd been in hundreds of times before, whether they were talking or watching a movie. Tonight, though, the position seemed more intimate.

They stayed that way for a while, Ella absorbing his touch, memorizing the way it felt simply to be with him. She'd lose that soon and she wanted to hang on to the memory forever.

"Not a bad dare," he said after a moment. "I'm surprised, though. A striptease doesn't seem like your kind of thing."

"No? What does?"

She felt his shoulders move in a shrug. "I don't

know. Running through the building in just a towel maybe."

"You can do that, too, if you want to."

He laughed. "No, thanks. All right. My turn. Truth or dare?"

"Truth," she said, then reconsidered. "No, wait. Dare."

He shook his head. "No way. You go with your gut. You picked truth, you're stuck with it."

"Fine. It'll be boring, though. You know I don't keep secrets from you."

He tilted his head so that he was looking at her more directly. In doing so, he brushed against her thighs, the pressure of the back of his head against her crotch near to driving her insane. "Except about your sex life with Tony, right?"

"Right. And that's because it's not your business." Not that she was withholding juicy details or anything. She and Tony had a rapport, a connection. But they didn't have wild monkey sex.

But they were a family. And that was more important than having mind-blowing sex. Sex and passion died, but the kind of connection she had with Tony survived and buoyed a marriage.

"Right. Not my business. Okay," Shane said, "here's my question."

"No. No way. You just asked me a question. Your turn is over, buddy."

He sat up, breaking contact with her legs, and she had to fight the urge to grab his shoulders and push him back down again.

"What? You're playing hardball?"

"You're the lawyer. You used your question. It's my turn now. Deal with it."

He held out a hand, signaling defeat. "Whatever you say, Counselor. The floor is yours."

"Good. Truth or dare?"

"Considering last time, I think I'm sticking with safety," Shane said. "Truth."

Dozens of possible questions whipped through her mind, but there was only one that made its way to her tongue. One treacherous question that she shouldn't ask, but she couldn't help herself. "The dance you did," she began, "did it turn you on?"

He didn't answer for a full beat, and she began to think he was going to take a pass on the question altogether. He surprised her, though, when he looked her straight in the eye and said, "Yes." Today, apparently, was going to be full of surprises.

"Oh." Should she ask what had turned him on about it? No. No, that would be stupid.

"You," he said.

"Excuse me?" Had she heard him right?

"It's your turn now. Truth or dare?"

"Oh." This time her voice was laced with disappointment. "Truth."

He shook his head and made a tsk-tsk noise. "I thought you had more guts, Davenport."

"Shove it, Walker. Ask your question and quit stalling."

"All right. Are you coming home to visit me at Christmas?"

She tensed, then turned away from him; turned away from the question. "I am home."

"I mean Texas."

"Shane, you know I—"

He didn't let her finish, though. He reached out and took her hands in his. "This isn't about your mom, El. It's about us. Are you going to come visit or not?"

"This is my home now." She said the words, but this time they seemed to come out with less force than she intended. "You can come visit here."

"You know I won't be able to. You'll be on break. I'll be working."

"I may be working, too," she said, and a wide smile split her mouth.

He stared at her a minute, absorbing her news. "Wait. You mean you—"

She broke him off with a vigorous nod. "Uh-huh. I got it! I got the internship."

He reached over, gathering her close for a hug. "El! That's awesome. I knew you would."

"Thanks. I'm blown away, of course. I haven't

even heard officially yet. Ronnie heard from the dean and she came to tell me."

"And you've gone this whole time without letting me know?"

She shrugged, feeling only a little guilty about that. She was already suffering from lust-induced guilt. She didn't have room for any more. "I was waiting for the right moment. And besides, you distracted me."

"Yeah? Well, now I'm even more glad I brought champagne. More?"

"Why not? I deserve it, right?"

"That you do." He leaned over and gave her a kiss on the cheek. Perfectly chaste, but the fire that ignited inside her was anything but. She fought the urge to turn her head, to press her lips to his and truly celebrate the moment.

So tempting. So very, very tempting...

"You really don't think you'll come back then? To Texas? Not even to see Alicia?"

Ella winced. Alicia—the maid who'd reluctantly become her nanny—had retired a few years ago. Ella might hate her parents and her hometown, but she didn't hate Alicia. The woman had been the closest thing to a mother she'd had.

If it had been up to Cecilia Davenport, Ella would have simply run wild. And without Alicia's influence, she really might have gotten in with a bad crowd. Drugs, dangerous sex, wild nights and fast cars. Why not? Isn't that what happened to kids with too much money and too little supervision?

But Alicia had stepped in, partly out of necessity and partly out of love. She'd never criticized Cecilia—at least not to Ella's face—but she'd taken up the slack. And to this day Ella could remember with stunning clarity how completely humiliated and ashamed she'd been when the apartment manager at Shane's apartment had called Ella's house and told Alicia—whom he'd assumed was her mother—that thirteen-year-old Ella had been tossing water balloons into the pool and he didn't appreciate the damage it could have caused to the drain system.

Alicia had sat her down, given her a lecture and then grounded her. She hadn't had any real authority, of course. Ella could have done whatever she wanted and just thumbed her nose at the maid. But she'd taken the punishment. Reveled in it, actually. And for the first time in her life she'd really and truly felt loved. For the first time she'd believed that she, like Cinderella, would come through a hideous childhood to find happily ever after waiting on the other side.

"I do miss her," Ella said. "But I hate going back there. You know that."

He nodded. "I know. And I understand. I just thought since I was going to be there now that maybe it would be a little less hideous."

Ella shrugged, not really wanting to talk about it. "Christmas is months away, Shane. My winter clothes are still in plastic tubs. Can't we talk about this later?" She managed to keep her voice calm, but inside she was screaming for him to change the subject. Because the subject was just too tough to bear.

"We can," he said. "But I'd like something to look forward to."

Ella bit her lip. The truth was she did want to go back, at least a tiny bit. She didn't want home or even Houston. But she wanted to see Alicia and she knew that by December she'd be going crazy to see Shane again. But she didn't want to get stuck in close quarters with him. This night was trying enough. And she didn't want to see her mother. The whole situation was one big balancing act. Add the holidays on top of that, and she was afraid everything would topple over under its own weight.

Better to go on her own terms if she was going to go at all. And better to go soon, because once her internship started, she intended to devote every ounce of energy to making a stellar impression on her advisor.

"Maybe next weekend," she said, taking the plunge. "I could help you unpack."

Shane stared at her, a question in his eyes.

"What?" she demanded. "Too soon?"

"Not at all. I was just wondering about Tony. He'll be back by then."

"True." She frowned. "But he'd probably rather me visit now than during the holidays. I mean, I've got family up here now." She thought of Leah and Matty. They were already talking about watching *White Christmas* and *The Bishop's Wife* while they all sat around and strung popcorn. Ella's mind was filled with images of happy family stuff—spending time with her new sisters and parents as they started new holiday traditions, drank eggnog and decorated the house.

"So you're not coming for the holidays," he said.

She frowned, irritated by the accusing tone in his voice. "I already told you. I'm not sure. I have to talk to Tony. And Texas isn't home anymore. New York is."

"Fair enough. In that case, I get to ask another question. Do you love Tony?"

"What? Sorry, Charlie, but it is *so* not your turn to ask a question. It's mine."

He shook his head. "You didn't answer about Christmas. I get another shot."

"I did so answer. I told you I didn't know. That's an answer."

He made a noise like a *Jeopardy!* buzzer. "Nope. Sorry. Thanks for playing."

"Shane…" Irritation flooded her voice, but she couldn't help it. He wasn't playing fair.

"Just answer the question, El. That's what this is, right? Truth or Dare? And it's not like it's a hard question, right? I mean, you're about to get engaged to the guy. We both know what the answer should be."

"Right," she said, fighting to put some force into her voice. "Of course I love him. It's just that it's a stupid, softball question. You *do* know the answer, so why even ask me?"

Her heart pounded in her chest, and she wondered if he could tell. But it wasn't a simple question. Love was so much more than an emotion. It was a whole life, and Shane obviously didn't get that.

"I know the answer," he said. "I'm just not sure you do."

"What's that supposed to mean?"

"Nothing," he said. "Not a thing."

"Dammit, Shane. I. Love. Tony. Just because *you* don't like him doesn't mean I can't love him."

"I never said I didn't like him."

"You didn't have to say anything. And it wouldn't matter even if you did. What *I* think matters, because I'm the one marrying him."

"Right."

She didn't even hesitate. She was on a roll. "And Tony is sweet and thoughtful and charming and he loves me, and I love him. Everything about him. His looks, his personality, his family. Leah and Matty are like sisters to me, and Tony's parents have welcomed me with open arms. I love them and they love me."

"I believe you love the whole Tony package,"

Shane said. "I'm just a little dubious about the man himself."

"Shane!" Her cheeks heated, her heart pounding against her rib cage. She wasn't certain which emotion was stronger, anger or mortification. Didn't matter. She was holding on to the anger and running with it. "You're on thin ice, buddy. Just because you're my best friend doesn't give you the right to—"

He held up a hand, silencing her. "You're right. You're right. I'm sorry. I crossed a line. Can I take it back?"

No, he couldn't. He'd pissed her off, questioned her choice of boyfriends. How could he take that back?

But this was Shane. Her fabulous, fun and loyal Shane. They'd never kept secrets or drawn lines before, so how could she fault him for tripping up? She couldn't and she didn't. So she nodded and was rewarded with a smile that spread slowly across his face, warming her as it grew.

"Okay," he said. "Let's skip the truth part. We're not having much luck in that area. How about a dare?"

"Sure. Why not?" Under the circumstances, performing a striptease seemed safer than talking about her love life.

"Right," he said. He topped up her champagne, and she drank it greedily.

"The thing we were talking about earlier. Exhibitionism. Public displays of affection. I dare you," he said. "I dare you to do it now."

"Do what?" She said the words slowly, afraid of jumping to conclusions and even more afraid that she was wrong.

So help her, she wanted to be right.

"Public displays of affection." His eyes glinted with mischief and this time with undeniable desire. "You said you wanted to. You said it's a fantasy." His green eyes pinned her, not letting her move or run. "So how about now? Do it with me."

She swallowed, not at all sure she could form words. "Another parting gift? Like the photographs?"

"If that's what you want to call it. Sure."

"Oh." Her stomach churned with nerves. She felt feverish. And wet. Dammit all to hell, she was actually wet.

The night around them seemed charged with electricity, and with a start she realized that the song playing on the radio was "Love the One You're With." At the moment that sounded like an absolutely fabulous idea.

"You're saying that I should make out with you. On the fire escape. In public."

"That's what I'm proposing, yes."

"Why?"

"You want the thrill. I'm your best friend. Isn't that what friends are for?"

"I…I'm not sure. I've never made out with any of my other friends." Didn't want to make out with any of her other friends. But she wanted Shane. She'd wanted him all day and now she could have him. Right there. Close enough to touch, to kiss…

"I just don't know. I've never done anything like that before."

"First time for everything," he said. He inched closer to her on the sofa, and she realized she was having a really hard time breathing.

"Shane…" But her protest was only for show. She already knew what she wanted, and that was his hands on her body, his mouth hard against hers. She didn't know if that made her a bad person or merely human, but she was certain that if Shane didn't touch her tonight, she'd regret it for the rest of her life.

She did want the experience he'd mentioned, wanted to know what it felt like to be so exposed to the world, to let the city envelop them and to simply lose herself in the heat. She told herself it was erotic curiosity, but the truth was it was so much more than that. If Shane had proposed making out in a dark closet, she knew she'd jump at that chance, too. Because the truth was she couldn't say no. Not now. She was too on fire, too curious and too downright horny to put the brakes on.

"Come on, Ella," he said, not realizing he'd already won. "I'm your best friend and I'm moving back to Texas in just a couple days. I won't be able to come over and commiserate if you have a bad day at school or a fight with Tony. Or if Tony isn't giving you everything you want in bed." He tucked a finger under her chin and lifted her face until she was looking right into his eyes. "The dare is my present to you. An unconventional present but yours if you want it. Do you?"

She couldn't speak, but she could nod.

So she did.

9

SHANE WAS PRETTY SURE HE was in heaven, but he still had to tread carefully. They were playing a dangerous game of tug-of-war here. She'd come closer to his side, all right, but had he pulled her? Or had she come of her own accord?

He didn't know and at the moment he didn't care. Instead he held her hand in his as he led her from the couch to the window. They climbed through, the metal grate vibrating underneath their feet as they crossed the short distance to the railing. Around them the candles stood like sentries, no longer illuminated, but the white wax glowed softly in the tiny bit of ambient light that had settled over the near-black city.

"Shane, maybe this isn't—"

He pressed a soft finger over her lips, not willing to hear any protests. "My present to you," he said.

And then he did what he'd been imagining for so long now. He kissed her.

When he did, he knew he'd been right all along—

he *was* in heaven. And in Ella's embrace he'd truly come home.

Her lips were soft beneath his. They'd always been one of her finest features, plump and kissable. He'd imagined this moment so many times, his mouth on hers, her lips parting to let him explore, but his fantasies hadn't matched the reality.

She tasted sweet, like champagne and strawberries, even though they'd eaten no fruit. He wanted to drink and eat from her lips, as if they could give him all the nourishment he'd ever need.

His hand was pressed against her back, but her hands didn't touch him. He urged her closer, and his cock twitched with the first stirrings of a massive hard-on.

Good God, if she wanted to stop, would he have the will to?

It was, thankfully, a question he didn't have to examine. At least not yet, because she moved closer, her mouth parting as her soft breasts pressed against his chest. She was warm and pliant and willing, and when she moaned, low and sexy, he wasn't sure how the hell he managed to keep from easing her to the ground and slamming hard and fast into her, right then, right there.

Her mouth opened with another low moan, and he slipped his tongue inside, meeting hers as they grappled with each other in a controlled passion. She wasn't giving anything away, and at the same time he knew everything. Most importantly, he knew that she wanted him, too. Maybe just for sex, maybe for more.

So help him, he intended to make it more.

SHE WAS KISSING HIM. HELL, more than that, she was fondling him.

Ella stroked her fingers over the back of Shane's neck, the pressure subtle, just enough to make sure that he didn't try to pull back. That he didn't seek to end this kiss of theirs.

At the moment Ella was pretty sure she'd die if he stopped kissing her.

His hands slid up her back under her shirt, the heat generated by the friction of skin against skin driving her absolutely, completely wild. She'd known this man for years, but somehow she'd never really known him until now. Certainly she'd never felt his skin burn under her touch or felt the trill of excitement race through him. Or felt his hard-on pressed against her belly.

Heady stuff, and she wanted it all so desperately she was almost ashamed. Almost. There wasn't really room in her head for any emotion other than want and need and the gentle mantra of *more* drifting through her mind.

"Is this what you wanted?" he murmured, his lips soft against hers.

She nodded, her mouth not quite able to form the word *yes*.

"But we're just kissing," he said, his voice both teasing and provocative. "Nothing particularly racy about doing that in public. Maybe you meant something with more of an X factor."

"X factor?" She spoke the words on a sigh, wanting his kisses, not his words.

"Exhibitionism, I mean. Something to up the thrill factor. Something like this maybe."

One hand snaked from behind her to ease between their bodies. She tensed with surprise and then her body tightened even more as his hand found her breast, his thumb flicking over her nipple through the thin material of her robe.

"Shane, I—"

"Hush," he whispered, then brushed his lips over hers. "Remember the fantasy. Someone's watching. Someone in one of those dark windows is looking out here and seeing you." He leaned close, his lips grazing her ear even as his thumb and forefinger played with her nipple. "Does that turn you on, El? Does it make you wet? Because that's the point, right? To get you hot? That's my present to you, and I want to give you the full experience."

As he spoke, his hand snaked down, slipping inside the robe. She wasn't wearing panties, and his fingertip brushed the soft skin just above her pubic hair.

She tensed, terrified he'd stop but more terrified he'd continue.

His fingers danced on her skin, heating her body but never actually easing lower. She squirmed under his touch, one hand still clutching his neck, the other flat against his chest. All she had to do was straighten her arm and she'd push him back. Then she could breathe. Get her head back on straight and tell him that this was too much, too fast. Her head was spinning.

But she didn't straighten her arm. Instead she closed her eyes and lost herself in the feel of his hand against her bare flesh, strung tight by the heady hope that his fingers would slip lower and lower.

They didn't, and she almost moaned in frustration. Instead his hand eased back up, this time sliding over the robe and then inside at the neck. He eased it over her shoulders and let it fall away so that it hung free, attached only by the loose tie around her waist.

The night was hot and humid. The rain had stopped, but it had done nothing to cool the city. The air felt sultry, sexy somehow, as if every molecule had joined with Shane to caress and tease her over-heated skin.

His hand slipped back down, tugged quickly at the sash. Ella gasped, as much from surprise as from the exhilarating sensation of being suddenly naked on her balcony, right there for all the world to see, with her pale blue robe pooled at her feet.

She opened her mouth to say something, though she wasn't sure what. Her head screamed that she should protest, but the rest of her body wanted simply to close her mind and lose herself in the moment.

She ended up saying nothing at all, instead giving in to the feel of Shane's mouth as he closed his lips over her breast, his hot tongue teasing her already sensitive nipple. She moaned and squirmed, desperate for more contact. If she'd been wearing her tight jeans, at least she'd be able to get some friction going in her crotch, maybe take some of the edge off the decadent pressure that was building in her veins. As it was, though, she was naked and needy.

From somewhere the thought came again that she should protest. She shouldn't let Shane do these things to her. The trouble was, at the moment she couldn't remember why not. Only that she wanted it. Needed it.

The feeling was so sensational, she didn't want it to end. And yes, there was a certain thrill attached to knowing that anyone looking out their window might see them. Might even be turned on by them.

Just the thought made her wetter, and she shifted, pressing her legs tight together. She was on the edge, right on the precipice, and all he had to do was touch her—just a featherlight touch against her crotch—and she knew she'd explode with an orgasm like nothing she'd had before.

"More." He ground out the word, his voice raw.

Oh, yes. She wanted to scream it. Wanted to pull him to her, feel him inside her. But it was hesitation that tinged her voice when she spoke. Hesitation and raw need. "God, Shane. I'm not sure. I'm—"

"Desperate," he said, his hand stroking down, his fingers finding her wet heat. She cried out, her body twitching as she writhed against his hand. And she knew that no matter what, this night wouldn't end without Shane inside her. "I can see it in your eyes, El," he added, his lips brushing her ear even as his finger played with her clit. "You want this. And so do I."

"I don't want to want it," she said. A useless protest but true.

In the background, Tina Turner's "What's Love Got To Do With It?" drifted out from the radio's speakers. He cocked his head toward the radio. "Tina understands."

"We're *friends*." Maybe if she forced herself to remember that, she could back away.

"Maybe more friends should fool around," he said.

"Shane, I think—"

He cut her off by pressing his mouth to her lips, then took her with a kiss so long and deep, she was sure she was going to lose herself. He pulled away slowly, and she wanted to whimper from the lost contact. Her lips were full and tender, and she wanted his touch again.

"Don't think," he said as he cupped her breasts. "Undress me, El. We're out here, under the sky. Let's finish what we've started."

Ella swallowed, but her fingers went to his jeans, fumbling with the button. *What they'd started...* They'd started fooling around. Hell, they'd started having sex. And even though she knew she ought to stop this right now, somehow she just couldn't. Somehow she *had* to have Shane. Now. Tonight.

If she didn't, this would always be hanging between them. Unfinished business. If she didn't, she'd always wonder.

But honestly those were just excuses. The real reason was that she was flat-out, boiling-over horny. She wanted him inside her more than she could remember wanting anything before.

She drew in a breath, her whole body seeming to shake in anticipation. "Tonight doesn't really feel real, does it?" she whispered. "It's almost magical."

He rolled her nipple between a thumb and forefinger as his other hand snaked down, teasing the soft skin on the inside of her thigh. Ella trembled under his touch and fought to keep her head clear. "There are always possibilities in the dark," he said. "And with a blackout..." He trailed off, and she looked up to see his wicked smile.

"It's like time has stopped," she said. "And nothing that happens tonight really counts."

She expected his easy agreement, but when it didn't come, she turned away from his touch, suddenly feeling exposed and just a little too daring.

Behind her she heard Shane sigh. "Truth or dare, Ella?"

She blew out a long breath. This was going to happen. She wanted his touch, even if only for tonight. And if he asked her that, she'd tell him. "Truth."

"We've known each other almost twenty years. You know everything there is to know about me. Except how I make love. Ever been curious?"

"I am now," she admitted. "But we're friends, Shane. Do we really want to change that?"

"*Would* it change that?"

"I—"

"It's a dare between friends, Ella. Not some sleazy proposition." He lifted his brows. "Unless you're chicken."

"I'm not chicken," she said. "But—"

"Tell you what," he said. "You ask. The ball's in your court."

"Me?" And then, when she realized what he meant, she nodded. She could walk away or she could take this forward.

As soon as they crossed the line, their relationship would change and there would be no going back. Was she willing to risk that?

But even as she asked herself the question, she had to acknowledge the tiny little voice in her head that pointed out that she'd already put everything between her and Shane on the line. And pulling back now wasn't going to change that in the slightest.

When the day had started, she would have said there was no way she'd see this through, but now every atom in her body screamed that she had to at least try or else she'd just dissolve in a heap of goo. Might as well get this thing between them out in the open before she spent the rest of her life dancing around intimate topics with her best friend.

She drew in a breath, then met his eyes. "Truth or dare, Shane?"

He met her eyes, his own dancing with anticipation. "Dare."

She drew in a breath, wanting it but still needing the courage to say it. And then quickly, before she could talk herself out of it, she said, "Make love to me, Shane. Here. Outside. With the world all around us."

She held her breath, fearful in spite of everything between them tonight that she'd gone too far. But the smile that crossed his face told her everything she needed to know, and when he silently pulled her into his arms, she practically melted against him.

He was brilliant in the way he touched her body.

His mouth teased her lips, dancing from there to her ear and lightly playing over her eyelids.

His hands stroked up to cup her bare breasts, his fingers finding her nipples and teasing them until she felt as though a strand of electricity had shot straight through her, connecting her nipples, her mouth and her clit.

Her body throbbed with need, and she shifted, spreading her legs to let him slide against her, his thigh pressed against her pubis. His hands slipped down, one gliding around to cup her rear.

She squirmed a bit, trying to increase the pressure of his thigh against her crotch. He shifted his leg, helping her out, and she just about melted with gratitude.

His lips grazed her ear, his soft breath on her tender flesh driving her wild. "Are you hot?" he whispered.

"Burning up," she admitted.

"Be right back."

And then he left her, and she was standing there outside, a gooey mass of lust and need. She cursed him softly, but he was back almost before the curse was out of her mouth.

"Where did you go?"

"The freezer. The ice hasn't melted yet."

"Shane, I meant I was *hot*. I didn't mean—"

"I know what you meant," he said, and there was such knowledge and raw maleness in his voice that she simply hushed up. "Close your eyes," he said, his voice broaching no argument.

She did, her mind too fogged with desire to let her

reconcile the Shane she knew with this aggressive, take-charge lover.

"Shane?"

"Shhh. Just wait."

"Shane, I—*oh!*" Something cold and wet pressed against her belly, and she arched her back, feeling her rear press against the warm, solid metal that surrounded the fire escape.

"Wait, wait," he whispered, his voice soft and reassuring. "Just relax."

She tried to, tried to focus on nothing but the sensation of ice against her burning hot skin. Tried not to think of who might be watching and then tried to think of exactly that. She shivered from the possibility as much as from his touch, and so help her, she slipped her own hand between her thighs without thinking.

"None of that," he whispered, pulling her hand away. "No taking the edge off. I'm the only one who gets to do that."

She groaned in frustration, but the sound was cut short, lost in her throat as Shane got busy with the ice cube. He drew a line from her belly button up between her breasts with the ice, leaving a long, wet trail that his tongue lapped up. He traced circles on her breasts with the ice, slower and slower as he got closer and closer to her tight, puckered nipple.

She whimpered, then cried out as his mouth closed over her. Heat on cold on hot, hot flesh.

Dear Lord, he was driving her crazy. And doing things in such a short time that she'd never done before with anyone at all.

He spent serious time on her breasts, making sure she was completely on fire and that every square inch of flesh had been fully attended to by his tongue. Then he took the wet remains of the cube and trailed it back down her belly.

He didn't slide the ice cube down between her legs, though. Just his hand, and the sensation of his chilled fingers sliding over her clit then slipping inside her until the digits were just as hot as she was just about drove her over the edge.

He slid his finger farther inside her, and she felt her body tighten around him, her hips thrusting against his hand, trying to urge him even deeper. He slipped out, and she moaned in protest, opening her eyes just long enough to see his little smile of satisfaction.

"Shane…"

He didn't even pretend to misunderstand. He thrust back inside her with two fingers, maybe three, she couldn't tell. All she knew was that he was filling her up and his thumb was flicking over her clit.

"Kiss me," she whispered, her eyes closed.

"Soon," he promised. His hands moved over her body, sure and possessive, as if they belonged there. As if she was his to do with whatever he wanted.

She lost herself, savoring the possibilities.

"Kiss me," he demanded.

She didn't hesitate, didn't even think. Just melted into him, her lips surrendering to his and her entire body longing to be kissed and touched just as thoroughly.

Their tongues danced together, his desperate heat consuming her. His hands were all over her, firing her body even more, though she never would have believed that was possible.

"You're beautiful, you know," he said, finally breaking the kiss. He urged them close to the candle and he inspected her in the flickering light, his finger tracing over her body.

He sank to his knees to continue the intimate inspection, then stopped when he got to the small scar on her lower belly, looking up at her with pain in his eyes. "I was so worried I'd lost you," he said, his finger tracing the length of the scar.

"You didn't lose me. You saved me." They'd been driving through upstate New York the year they'd moved there, and she'd started to feel terrible. He'd insisted on finding a hospital and had headed back toward the nearest city despite her protests that she wanted to see the countryside. Because he'd been an unwavering bastard who hadn't listened to a word she'd said, they'd been only five miles from the hospital when her appendix had burst.

He'd taken care of her then and all through her recovery. For that matter, she couldn't remember a time and couldn't imagine a future without Shane there watching out for her.

He didn't answer, but he did press a soft kiss to the scar. A series of little shocks shot through her, and she gripped the railing to steady herself. Good thing, too, because she became decidedly less stable as his kisses dropped lower and lower.

He slipped his hands between her thighs and urged her legs apart and then slowly and sensually he laved her sex with his tongue. Ella's knees went weak, and she was absolutely certain that if he didn't stop, she was going to fall over, but she was just as certain that she might keel over and die if he *did* stop.

Except that wasn't really what she wanted. No, as fabulous as his mouth against her was, those intimate kisses weren't what she really wanted. She wanted— no, *needed*—this man inside her.

"Shane…" The voice that came out of her was weak like a kitten and full of protest.

He stopped and stood up, the expression on his face making it absolutely clear that he knew exactly what she wanted. She wasn't surprised. They'd never had to use words where important things were concerned. Why would they start now?

"You're sure?"

She didn't answer with words, just reached again for the button on his jeans and started to fumble with it, finally getting it free, then starting to work on the zipper.

His hands closed over hers. "Better let me do that. I don't want to injure anything important and you look a little shaky."

"If I am, it's your fault."

"Good."

He finished undressing and then he stood there, naked in front of her, hard and lean and so very ready.

He leaned down and pulled a condom packet from the back pocket of his jeans. She frowned, something striking her as off, but she couldn't quite think what it was. For that matter, she couldn't quite think…

"You're sure about this?" he asked as he ripped open the condom.

"You already asked me that," she said. She drew in a breath and looked him straight in the eye. "I'm sure. Don't ask me again."

SHANE WASN'T ABOUT TO ASK again. As soon as the question had slipped out of his mouth, he'd regretted it, fearing that she'd change her mind and shut the whole thing down.

That she hadn't was a gift. And he had no intention of letting her take that gift back.

With one fluid motion he pulled her close, then moved them both around so that she was pressed up against the railing. He reached between her legs, thrilled by the wet heat he found there, and dammit all, he couldn't wait.

He spread her legs, then grabbed her ass and lifted her up. She let out a startled little moan but didn't hesitate to wrap her legs around his waist. Then he slid into her, losing himself in her wet heat.

She grabbed his shoulders, her fingernails digging in, her body insisting without words that he pound harder, faster.

He didn't argue. And he thrust into her again and again until, too soon, she cried out and thrashed against him. Her body tightened, milking him, and his own body exploded in response.

Moments later, she slid down him, and he sank, limp and sated, to the grating beside her, pulling her close to him and wrapping his arms around her. They were on his jeans, the only barrier between them and the hard, rough iron. For Shane, though, they might as well have been on a lush bed surrounded by pillows. Anywhere that Ella was in his arms was heaven to him.

"That was nice," she whispered.

"Very."

"Do you think—" She cut herself off, burying her face against his chest as if she'd suddenly gone shy.

He laughed. "Do I think that anyone saw us? I don't know." He shifted, bringing his mouth as close to her ear as possible. "Maybe we should put on an encore performance." He trailed a finger up her thigh, enjoying the way she stretched and mewled like a kitten. "You know, just in case someone out there missed our fifteen minutes of fame."

"Isn't that cheating? Stealing more than our fifteen minutes?"

"We took it pretty fast, El. I think between the two of us we should have another fifteen minutes of fame coming to us."

She shifted, looking up at him with narrowed, amused eyes. "We did take it rather fast and furious, didn't we?"

"I blame that on you, sweetheart. But I can take it slow now. As slow as you like." As he spoke, he stroked his hand down, his palm cupping her sex and one finger slipping inside her heat. God, he was in heaven, living a fantasy. And the only thing that could make this moment better would be to make it permanent.

"You're very persuasive," she murmured, her voice thick.

"That I am."

She rolled over into his arms then, her breasts pressed against his chest. He leaned in to kiss her, desperate for the feel of her mouth against his once again. He'd known for months that he wanted her, but he'd never imagined just how responsive—how hot—she would be in his arms. And he'd imagined some pretty red-hot moments...

"It *is* only fair," she said, a sexy smile playing at

her mouth. "I mean, I'd hate to disappoint our adoring fans."

And then she moved even closer, and he held his breath, waiting for her touch.

It didn't come.

Instead she pulled back, her brow furrowed and her hand on his shoulder. "Did you hear that?"

"What?" He hadn't heard a thing. But just as he was about to ask again, the pounding started up again.

"Ella? Ella, are you awake?" a female voice called.

Shane scowled. The last thing in the world he wanted was a third wheel. But as he got up to follow Ella to the door, he couldn't help but notice that Ella looked just as irritated by the interruption.

"Don't go," he whispered.

"I have to," she said. "It's Marjorie. She might need help. I can't just ignore her."

He nodded, then leaned back to let her pass. She called a quick greeting toward the door as she climbed back inside the apartment, then started pulling on her clothes. Still on the fire escape, Shane also got dressed.

He took a last glance around. The area had been awash with sensuality mere moments before. Now it simply looked like a fire escape.

He understood why Ella had pulled away. He even loved her for it, her kindhearted nature.

But that didn't change the fact that, for the moment at least, the magic had faded. And Shane could only stand there, hoping to hell they'd be able to get it back.

10

ELLA'S ENTIRE BODY TINGLED, and for half a second she actually considered not answering the door. But it was Marjorie, and her neighbor was one of the most easily rattled women Ella had ever met. If Marjorie was at the door, chances were she was scared or had locked herself out or was otherwise experiencing some kind of crisis, real or perceived.

"Ella?"

"Coming, Marjorie. Just give me a sec."

She took a quick look behind her and saw Shane climbing through the window. He was dressed now, just as she was. And by all appearances everything was back to normal.

Except, of course, it wasn't normal at all.

She took a deep breath, patted her hair and adjusted her clothes, then flipped the locks and pulled the door open.

"Ella!" Marjorie said, rushing inside holding a squatty candle sporting a puny flame. Marjorie was twice Ella's age, but you couldn't tell it from the woman's bounce and energy level. And scattered nature. She was a receptionist at a midtown law firm, and Ella had to wonder how she kept the job. The odds that she ever once got a phone message correct were slim to none.

Marjorie shot a look toward Shane, and her eyebrows lifted dramatically. "Oh! I didn't realize you were…*busy.*"

Ella's face heated, and she turned quickly, wondering if Shane had decided not to put his shirt back on after all. But no, he was fully dressed and standing by the table, a champagne flute in his hand.

And, okay, yes, he did look completely sexy and hot, but that didn't mean Marjorie needed to jump to conclusions. Even if the conclusions were correct.

Marjorie leaned in closer. "I'm so happy for you two. I was wondering if you'd ever—"

"Marjorie!" Ella hissed. "We're just friends. He got stuck here during the blackout. We've been, um, hanging out." And then, just so that her neighbor would be sure to believe her fabrication, she swept her arm out, indicating the small apartment. "You're welcome to join us if you want."

A flicker crossed Shane's face—disappointment? irritation?—but Ella ignored it. There *wasn't* anything going on between them. Nothing except two friends doing a little male-female exploration. A clearing of the air between them. A shift in circumstances, certainly, but they were hardly pairing up for good. She already had her life planned out, and while Shane was in it, he wasn't cast in the role of husband. He knew that. He'd even said as much. Well, sort of, anyway.

"Oh, no, no," Marjorie said. "I couldn't. But you two have fun. I just came to borrow a flashlight. My candles are on their last legs, and I hate the thought of being in the pitch-black."

"I'm so sorry," Ella said. "We couldn't find them anywhere. Do you want to take a few candles?"

"Oh, sweetie, no. I couldn't take your candles. You need them. I'll just go see if Mr. Kramer upstairs has any."

"Don't be silly," Ella said. "It's the middle of the night. He's probably sound asleep. We can spare a few."

"I just wouldn't feel right, dear. I should probably just blow out my candle and go to bed anyway. It's just that the city is never this quiet. I tried to sleep, but it gives me the willies. And sitting up in the dark…well, I'm not sure I can."

Ella drew a breath, not looking at Shane as she said, "If you're nervous, you really can stay here with us." She hoped Marjorie would say no, but she had to make the offer. She wouldn't feel right otherwise.

Behind her she could hear Shane moving around, probably furious with her. Furious and hurt. Well, they could talk about all this tomorrow, after Marjorie was gone and they had clearer heads.

And frankly, as much as she'd been enjoying the evening's turn of events—understatement of the century—the fact remained that they were probably better off with a chaperone.

"Oh, dear. I don't want to put you out. Are you sure—"

"Found them!"

Ella whirled around to find Shane on his hands and knees, backing away from the chest of drawers, a flashlight clutched in each hand and one tucked in under his chin.

"Ella said she was certain she had flashlights," he said. "I guess we just missed these." He passed them to Marjorie with a chivalrous flourish. "These should keep you in light through the rest of the night."

"Oh, you two, this really is wonderful. And you're sure you don't mind? Do *you* have a flashlight?"

"I had several," Ella said, wondering where on earth Shane had found the wayward flashlights.

"Only found three," he said. "Is that enough?"

"I'm sure," Marjorie said. "Don't you worry about me. I think I'll pull out the telescope I inherited from my father. Not much use for it in the city, but tonight's so clear. I've never tried it out before, so it should be fun." She flashed Ella a motherly smile, coupled with the tiniest gleam in her eye. "I guess it's just a night for new things all around."

Ella swallowed, her cheeks instantly flaming. Fortunately it was dark by the door, and she doubted that Marjorie saw. "Well, have fun," Ella said.

"Absolutely. You, too."

"We will," said Shane, and then he was ushering Marjorie out the door with just a bit more speed than good manners required.

He shut the door, set all three locks, then turned to her.

"Sorry," she said. "She's been a dear to me ever since I moved in. I had to help her out, invite her in."

"I know," he said. "I like Marjorie, too. And she adores you." The social niceties taken care of, he shifted gears, his expression changing from one appropriate for the general public to the heated face of a man interested in only one very private thing. "So," he said, "where were we?"

For half a second she considered protesting. Marjorie's interruption was the perfect time to insert some distance and common sense. But despite the splash of cold water that had been Marjorie's knock, Ella still wasn't quite free of the spell Shane had cast. In other words, damn her, she still wanted him.

She knew in her head that she shouldn't, but she'd had that argument with herself earlier and she didn't see any reason to rehash. They'd already crossed the line from purely platonic to…something else. In the harsh light of day, they'd have to figure out how they were going to approach their friendship after he'd slipped his hands into her panties. But they were grown, mature people. They'd work it out. And that was a problem best solved during the daytime.

Now, in the velvety darkness, working out their friendship wasn't her prime concern. Feeling Shane inside her, *that* was all she wanted.

And so she drew in a breath, snaked her arm around his neck and pressed her lips to his. The kiss was long and deep, and when she pulled back, she saw the expression of heated desire in his beautiful eyes.

"I think we were somewhere about here," she whispered.

"I think you're right," he said, then pulled her close for another kiss.

When they broke apart, he pushed away with a devious grin. "So what do you want to do now? Maybe play some checkers? Maybe a nice game of chess? Or how about a rousing game of Go Fish?"

She nipped at his shoulder, then slid her hand down his pants, cupping his cock through the thin material of his briefs. "I'll go fish," she said. "Oh, and look, I think I've caught something."

He laughed and pulled her down on the couch with him, then started to kiss and tickle her at the same time. She squealed and kicked and giggled. "Stop! No fair! You know how ticklish I am."

"Eet is true," he said. "I know all zee secrets of zee lady. Do as I ask or suffer zee punishment."

"You're a freak. You know that, right?" But she was grinning broadly, thinking that she was actually having fun and fooling around at the same time. Not that sex with Tony wasn't fun, but this was…silly and teasing and natural. But of course it would be. Shane was her friend. He knew her sense of humor.

"Eet is time for me to pull out my chamber of torture," he said.

"The only thing you're torturing is that accent." She rolled off the couch, then watched as he pushed the coffee table aside and pulled the futon out into a full bed.

She grabbed some sheets off the armoire and tossed them on top of the mattress, not bothering to tuck in the corners.

"Lie down," he said, then waggled his eyebrows like a cartoon villain. "Lie down naked."

She lifted an eyebrow. "Just what exactly do you have in mind, buddy?"

"If I told you, it wouldn't be a surprise, now would it?"

"Is this a surprise I'll like?"

"That's my plan," he said, his voice pitched low. She licked her lips, feeling more than a little nervous but turned on at the same time. The candles inside had burned down, but they still flickered, casting an orange glow over them and making shadows play across Shane's gorgeous face.

He leaned against the armoire, arms crossed in front of him, and watched as she undressed. Instinctively she turned away, giving him her back.

"No way, El. I want to watch."

She closed her eyes, imagining each bit of clothing coming off, one by one, as Shane's gaze caressed her. Yeah, she could do that.

Slowly she turned around, then slipped out of the tank top once again. She gave it a little spin as it came off her right arm, then sent it flying. It landed on his head with aplomb, and she laughed. "Ba-dum, ching!"

"Not bad," he said. "Keep going."

She licked her lips, then untied her yoga pants, loosening the waist enough so that they fell around her ankles as she did a little shimmy. "I thought strip-teases were your territory."

"I'm expanding your horizons," he said. "Keep going. The view from my side of the room is fabulous and just keeps on getting better."

She turned and wriggled her butt as she eased out of her panties, tossing them at him, as well. She looked over her shoulder at him, wondering if he could tell that she was totally wet.

"What do you want, El?" From the tone of his voice she knew he was aware just how hot she was.

"Touch me," she said. She moved toward him, but he held out a hand and shook his head, just slightly but enough to stop her in her tracks.

"No. Get on the bed."

"Yeah? And where are you going to be?" she asked as she climbed onto the bed.

"Right behind you," he said. But she noticed that wasn't quite right. First he went to her armoire and pulled down the hatbox she used to store all of her scarves. He opened it, pulled out four and waved them at her.

"On your back, Ella," he said. "And spread your arms and legs."

SHANE HELD HIS BREATH, wondering if she'd let him take it that far. If she'd really surrender to him so completely. If she'd really let herself be completely his.

He toyed with the idea of just telling her that he wanted her, and not just tonight. Not just for sex. But no. He couldn't lay it on the line until all the pieces were in place. If he confessed, she'd only deny her feelings.

No, he needed to make sure her body was completely his before her mind got involved in the argument. That way, at least, he'd have a chance.

He wasn't there yet, but he was close. Bits of her

shield were falling away, and she was forgetting why she fought so hard to stay with a man she didn't truly love. He could take her the rest of the way. He knew it.

He knew he could do it, because he'd already done it on the fire escape. He'd felt her give herself to him, and it had been a piece of heaven.

Still, the specter of Tony hung over them. Ella was determined to be with the man even though she should by all rights and reason be with Shane.

If he really believed that Ella loved Tony, he wouldn't press the issue. But he didn't believe it. She was his soul mate, and he was hers. Tony was a nice enough guy—well, actually, Shane thought he was an ass, but Ella liked him. Nice wasn't what mattered. Love did. And Ella didn't really love Tony.

At least, that's what Shane kept telling himself. Because if she *didn't* love Tony, then Shane was rescuing her. If she *did* love Tony, then maybe he was a shit for trying to seduce her away from her boyfriend.

It was a possibility he didn't like to consider, so he didn't. As a lawyer, he saw the end result and he went after it. And the end result here was Ella and their life together. And to Shane that was something worth fighting for.

In front of him she'd climbed onto the bed, had spread her arms, but her legs were together, knees bent, her ankles back near her butt. A pretty picture to be sure, but not the one he wanted. Not raw enough, and he needed her raw.

He made a rough motion with his hands. "Spread your legs, Ella. I want you to spread your legs."

He held his breath. Moment-of-truth time. And then, as she shifted, split open her thighs for him, his cock stiffened and his body fired. Oh, yes. She'd be his all right. She already was. She just didn't realize it.

"Close your eyes," he insisted, and she did without question. For a second he felt a twinge of guilt. He was her best friend, and she trusted him, opening herself up to him in ways neither of them would have imagined even a few short days ago.

He'd stacked the deck in his favor, no doubt about that. Did that make him a cheater or just a man in love?

He wasn't sure, but as he looked at Ella's smooth body laid out before him like an offering, he decided it didn't matter. Whatever motivations had brought them here were in the past now. Now it was just him and Ella.

She started a little when he touched her foot, her teeth working her lower lip as he secured both ankles and her left wrist to the slatted frame of the futon bed. When he took her last free wrist, though, she whispered, "Shane…"

He pressed a kiss to her lips. "Shhh. Do you trust me?"

"Yes." No hesitation. Just *yes,* and that one simple word sliced through his soul, red-hot and dangerous.

He stepped back from the bed and looked at her, simply watching the way the light played over her body, turning him on. He was tempted just to stand there looking at her, lost in this moment when she belonged completely to him.

A nice thought maybe, but one that wasn't about to happen. No way was he going to look but not touch. He wanted this too badly, wanted *her* too badly. Even after losing himself in her less than an hour ago, he still hadn't had his fill. He needed more. He needed to claim her.

Raw lust poured through him. Lust and jealousy. How could she want Tony? She didn't love him. He knew that. There was no way she could open herself up to Shane the way she did unless she loved *him*.

He knew it. So why didn't Ella?

"Shane?" Her soft voice, so filled with need, drifted to him, and he shoved all thoughts of jealousy aside. This moment alone filled his mind. This moment, this woman and a bone-deep hunger.

"I'm coming," he said, his voice little more than a growl.

He straddled her, his cock pressing against her soft belly. She gasped and arched up against him, as desperate for him as he was for her.

But this time wasn't about fast. This time was about slow. He wanted everything from her. And he started with her fingers, suckling each one in turn, drawing them into his mouth as he imagined her drawing him into her body.

She made a little moaning sound, and he tilted his head. Her eyes, warm and dreamy, met his. "No, no," he whispered, then slid off just long enough to take one more scarf and tie it gently over her eyes.

"You're all mine," he whispered. "And right now you see and feel only what I tell you."

SHE LIKED THIS.

Ella's mind was mush and not really up to forming complicated or poetic thoughts, but the one thing she knew for certain was that she liked this. Plain and simple. Liked having Shane take charge. Liked feeling special and cherished and the center of his universe.

And yeah, she liked the way she felt totally turned on.

Most of all she liked how relaxed she felt, even while every atom in her body hummed on the edge of desperation and wild abandon. She'd never, ever, done this with anyone else—let a man tie her up and blindfold her and have his way with her totally—and she couldn't imagine doing it with anyone else. But this was Shane and, yeah, she trusted him.

He wouldn't take it too far or hurt her or embarrass her. Just the opposite, in fact. This was all about making her feel totally amazing.

Which, as it happened, was how she felt now that he'd returned to suckling on her fingers, the gentle pressure igniting a live wire that seemed to spread throughout her entire body. She moaned and strained against the silky bonds, not wanting to be free so much as wanting to touch him back.

He made a soft noise, gently chastising her, then continued to explore every inch of her with his mouth. Everywhere his lips touched, her body seemed to catch fire, and she shimmied on the bed, desperate for his hands to slip between her legs— desperate even just to close her thighs together tight and squeeze, but she couldn't. She was wide open and at his mercy, and that only turned her on all the more.

She was just about to beg when she felt the weight on the bed change and his lips lift from her skin. Then his knees pressed on either side of her as he slid down, repositioning himself over her. She made a soft sound of surprise mixed with hope and then lifted her hips off the bed, embarrassingly needy but really not caring. She could feel him right *there,* his cock pressed against her, the teasing pressure making her even more wet. She jerked, a spastic reaction, desperate to draw him inside her.

And Shane, bless the man, understood. With one quick thrust he entered her, groaning with pleasure as he did. And now, with her best friend deep inside her, she could only think that this was like something out of an erotic fantasy. Actually it *was* her erotic fantasy.

The thought sent a wild trill of pleasure coursing through her body, and she arched her hips, wanting more of this man who was her fantasy come to life. In her whole life she'd never acted on her fantasies. But now she was. They could make love all night, take each other in ways she'd only imagined. She could tell him all her fantasies—the ones she could never tell Tony but just her best friend—and he could make them a reality.

Dear Lord, he *was* making them a reality.

The ability to think faded as they moved together rhythmically, her body arching up to meet his, his kisses wild and hot. And only one coherent thought edged through her addled brain as the orgasm whisked her away: they *fit*.

Hell, they always had.

She should have known they'd fit together so well as lovers. It should have been obvious.

Instead she'd been swept away by a delicious surprise. And for the moment, at least, she couldn't have been happier.

"WE SHOULD SLEEP," SHANE said as he gently untied the scarves that bound her.

Ella shook her head. Every minute they slept was a minute they lost together. And she couldn't bear to lose even a second. "Do you really want to sleep?"

"No," he admitted. "But I didn't want you to think I was a sex fiend or something."

She laughed and rolled over to snuggle against him, relishing the warmth of his skin and the musky scent of sex. "Too late."

"You're not sore?"

"A little. But I like it. I feel taken."

He propped himself up on his elbow and looked at her, his expression a bit more serious than she would have expected. "Have I taken you away?"

"Of course," she said. "You've taken me places I've never been before." An honest answer, but somehow she had the feeling she hadn't really answered his question. And it wasn't a question she wanted to examine too closely because she didn't want to go where it could lead—*to Tony*.

The truth was she felt totally at ease with Shane. Happy and comfortable hanging out or having sex or even being tied up and totally vulnerable. She'd never felt that way with Tony. Never felt as though if she didn't touch him or he didn't touch her, she might die.

With Tony she'd never really felt drawn to sex. To his life, yes, but not to sex. And that little tidbit of reality made her sad. Sex wasn't the sum total of a relationship, of course. And passion faded, she knew that. Sex wasn't what made a stable marriage or even a happy one.

She couldn't help but want that wildness and she had it right now with Shane.

She wanted to hang on to that feeling for as long as she could. Wanted to keep him with her and draw every memory she could from this day, because soon he'd be going to Texas and she'd be going back to Tony and everything would return to normal. More or less, anyway.

"Ella?" He stroked a finger down her cheekbone. "Have I lost you?"

She shook her head, hoping to push the melancholy away. "I was just thinking about how different you are tonight."

"This is me, Ella. This is the same me who's been beside you all your life."

"Then I wonder if that 'same me' would like to play out another little fantasy of mine," she teased. "You brought up the piece about the photographs, but there's another one that's always intrigued me. I told you about it once. Do you remember?"

"The mysterious stranger," Shane said with a nod. "Yeah. I, um, brought a modern-day version of that story, too. For your paper, I mean."

"Yeah?" She smiled, intrigued. The end result of his reading of the photographer's story had been more than satisfactory. "Maybe we should read it. You know, chalk it up to studying?"

The scenario was common in erotica, but it was still one of her favorites: a woman, possibly married, frustrated with her current situation. She'd never cheat, but when faced with a mysterious stranger—

She realized with a start that, tonight at least, Shane *had* been as mysterious as any stranger. A Shane she barely knew had come to her and taken her to bed.

"You want me to play the dark, sexy stranger?" he asked.

She grinned. "Isn't that what we've been doing tonight?"

He shook his head, the hardness in his face surprising her. "No." He said the word with such force, she scooted back a bit.

Then he closed his eyes and shook his head. This time he spoke more softly, but he said the same thing. "No."

"Shane?" Something had pushed a button, but she wasn't sure what.

"I don't want to be a stranger to you, Ella. Not even pretend. Everything we've done tonight, we've done with our eyes open."

"I…" She trailed off, suddenly flustered, the veneer of fantasy starting to crack around her. "I mean, sure. Of course."

He shook his head, and she could see the frustration roll off him in waves. "I'm sorry," he said, reaching for her hand. "I didn't mean to snap. And I know just the way to lighten the mood."

"Yeah?"

"Let's play a game."

"A game?"

"Trust me," he said. Then he smiled mischievously. "We're playing Strip Go Fish."

"Strip Go Fish," she repeated, unable to hide her amusement. "But we're already naked."

He rolled over to the edge of the bed and tossed her clothes toward her. "Put them on," he said. "And then we can get naked all over again."

11

THEY LAY SPOONED TOGETHER, the Go Fish game having only stripped them both of their shirts. After that Shane hadn't been able to stand it any longer. He'd pulled her knit pants off, seen that she hadn't bothered with panties and slid into her while she'd been on her hands and knees.

He could still feel the way her breasts felt in the palms of his hands as he'd thrust, the soft curves of her ass pressing against him as he lost himself deep inside her. He'd come hard and fast, and so help him, he was ready to go again.

With Ella he always seemed to be ready to go again.

"What are you thinking?" she murmured, snuggling up closer.

He told her and she laughed. "You're insatiable," she said.

"Apparently so," he said. In the background, "You Shouldn't Kiss Me Like That" played, and Shane let the words flow over him, one thought pounding through his head—he and Ella had to figure out a way to make this last, because he couldn't bear to be just friends. She'd kissed him "like that," and he damn sure hoped she'd meant it. Because in his mind she was his. And no matter what, he intended to claim her.

"I think it's my turn," she whispered, her voice playful.

She rolled him over onto his back and straddled him, her fingers trailing over his abdomen, her rear right above his cock so that she rubbed against him when she moved, making him hard all over again.

He reached up, rubbing her stomach, her breasts, moving his hands to span her waist. Had he already done it? Had he already claimed her? Surely he must have. How could she be this free with him otherwise? How could they be so intimate if she simply planned to call a halt when he went back to Texas?

The thought cheered him, but he couldn't analyze it too closely because she lifted her hips and, with a cry of pleasure, impaled herself on him. And then, of course, he could think of nothing except the woman on top of him and the way she was riding him, drawing him out, urging the universe to explode, with him right there in the center of it.

ELLA HAD COLLAPSED AGAINST Shane, totally spent, totally sore and totally satisfied. Now her thoughts drifted as he breathed deeply in sleep beside her.

She'd called the shots that last time, taking charge and riding him to an orgasm that had just about shattered them both. And once again she was struck by how she'd never done anything like that with Tony. They'd tried, actually, but they just didn't quite fit, and somehow they always ended up with her on her back and him thrusting from above her. Nice enough but not like this. With Shane it was just...*wow.*

More thoughts of Tony filled her mind, along with a deep guilt. She eased off Shane and rolled over, snuggling up against him. His arm went around her automatically, and she welcomed it, taking comfort from his touch even though he was the reason she felt uncomfortable in the first place.

The truth was, there had to be something missing in her relationship with Tony. And something more than just sex. She wasn't the cheating type. She'd never cheated on a boyfriend—well, not before tonight— and the thought had never even entered her mind.

But with Shane they'd practically fallen into it. Of course, she'd been primed by that little fantasy in the library. And the night had been perfect for seduction. First the fancy candlelight dinner, then the blackout and even more candles since her flashlights had gone AWOL. And then—

Wait just a minute!

She turned over, sitting up with a start as the realization hit. Shane had known exactly where to find flashlights when Marjorie had come over. And he'd had a condom in his back pocket—not in his wallet, just loose in his pocket. And the candlelight dinner. And the erotica selections he'd just happened to bring.

She'd been an idiot not to notice before. They hadn't fallen in together as she'd thought. No, she'd been pushed—and hard—by Shane.

Dear Lord. He'd tricked her. Manipulated her. He was her best friend and yet he'd actually had the balls to do that to her.

Everything she'd thought she knew seemed to shatter, and she rolled onto her side, moving away from the heat of Shane's naked body beside her. With a frown she reached for her robe, suddenly wanting to be covered up. She slipped her arms through the sleeves and stood up, haphazardly knotting the belt as she made her way into the bathroom.

The one candle they'd set up in there still burned, and she closed the door behind her, then slid down the door until her legs were pulled up in front of her and she could press her forehead against her knees.

He'd lied to her.

This evening hadn't just happened. It hadn't been just a case of two friends sparking together. The whole evening had been a full-fledged, all-out assault. The romantic dinner, the erotica open to all the right pages, the hidden flashlights to force the candlelight issue. Hell, if she didn't know better, she'd say that Shane had engineered the blackout. Instead he'd just gotten supremely lucky.

She closed her eyes at the poor choice of words. He'd gotten lucky, all right. And if she was being fair, she had to admit that she'd enjoyed it. No, it was more than enjoyed. He'd absolutely, totally blown her away.

But she never—ever—would have slept with Shane under normal circumstances. He'd stacked the deck. And while that might be flattering if she were unattached, the fact was that he'd done it knowing full well that she was about to be engaged to another man.

She felt like a total slut.

And Shane? Well, at the moment he was the biggest jerk she knew.

Shane was sound asleep, and at the moment she really didn't want to wake him up. She couldn't deal with talking to him right now. For that matter, she really couldn't deal with anything.

She felt itchy, dirty and uncomfortable in her own skin.

She stood up and wandered through the apartment, finally grabbing the box that held her loose photographs. She took it, then headed back into the bathroom, the only place where she could really have any privacy.

An hour before, she couldn't imagine Shane leaving, now she wanted him gone. She needed him at a safe distance so she could get her head clear. But he was in her bed, and she was stuck in the bathroom. Thank goodness he was flying out in a couple days. He'd be gone and she'd be left with Tony.

And that was what she wanted, wasn't it?

Of course it was.

She started the water running in the tub, then got in when it was only half-full. She soaped up completely, overcome with the need to be totally clean. Then she lay back and stared at the ceiling.

After that got old—her thoughts were too wild and she really didn't want to think about anything too deeply—she reached for her towel and dried her hands, then sat up. She'd put the box on the little table near the tub and now she pulled out the photos one by one. She held them up, careful not to get them wet, and examined each in turn. Pictures of Tony and Leah and Matty. Tony's dad and mom on a picnic. And even Shane's earlier accusation—that she was marrying the family, not Tony—couldn't take away the strong family ties the photos conveyed.

"Bastard," she whispered, then grabbed a bottle of shampoo and hurled it at the door. Plastic, it merely banged against the wood then dropped harmlessly to the floor. A bit unsatisfying, but it wasn't shampoo she wanted to break, it was Shane's conniving head.

He'd been playing her even though he knew how happy she was with Tony. Knew how much she wanted a family and how thrilled she was to have one with a man she loved. Why on earth would her best friend try to screw her over? Try to mess with her mind—not to mention her body—the way Shane had?

It wasn't fair, and right at the moment she hated him for it.

SHANE ROLLED OVER, ONLY half-asleep. His body was limp with exhaustion, but at the same time he felt more alive and more full of energy than he could ever remember feeling. Ella had that effect on him. Just being around her was like a shot of energy to him. Being inside her was like…

Well, it was like mainlining caffeine while drinking champagne. Which really made no sense, he realized, but since he wasn't even really awake yet, he didn't care.

Ella would get a kick out of it, though, especially with her Starbucks addiction and love of bubbly.

He rolled over to tell her, only to realize she wasn't there. In fact, the spot next to him was cool—or as cool as could be expected without air-conditioning.

He ran his fingers through his hair and sat up, his head spinning slightly. He must have dozed off after all. Which was fine, except that he'd wanted to wake up in Ella's arms. For that matter, he'd wanted never to leave her arms again.

She was, of course, in the bathroom. That was

one of the benefits of a tiny apartment—you always knew where your housemate was. And he headed over and tapped softly at the door. No answer. He tapped again. "Ella."

"Do you need in here?"

He cocked his head, examining the wooden door. That wasn't the answer or the tone he'd been expecting. "No, I'm fine. Are *you* fine?"

No answer, and he didn't like the way the silence sounded.

He twisted the knob without hesitation, thinking that she was sick and that he had to get in there and take care of her, but then stopped and called, "El, come on, sweetheart. What's wrong?"

"I'm not your sweetheart, Shane," she said, her voice lower and sadder than he could ever remember hearing. "And pretty much everything is wrong. So just go away for a bit, okay. I want to think."

Well, shit.

He turned around, looking back at the bed, all rumpled and inviting. For a few hours there everything had been perfect, and he wasn't willing to let go of that. He sure as hell wasn't letting go without a fight.

"Ella," he called again. "Come on out. We need to talk."

"We damn sure do," came the reply. And then nothing. He waited for the knob to turn, but it never did.

"Ella!"

Nothing.

He knocked on the door, but still nothing.

Raking his fingers through his hair, he turned a slow circle, looking at the apartment in the dim glow of the few remaining candles and the sun, which was just beginning to rise outside the windows. Dammit all, she might be his best friend and the love of his life—his soul mate, even—but she could drive him crazy faster than any person he knew.

"El?" He tried one last time. "Come out now and let's talk. Whatever's bugging you, this isn't the way to deal with it."

"Whatever's bugging me?" she repeated. "Believe me, Shane. I'm well justified in being bugged. I'm even justified in being totally, completely, one hundred percent pissed off. And if anyone should know that, it's you."

He was reaching the end of his temper. Whatever issue she had, it had to have stemmed from their extracurricular activities this evening. Which meant that she was just as complicit as he was, and he wasn't about to just sit there and let her sulk about some imagined injury inflicted by him.

He lifted his hand to pound on the door, not expecting to be let in but just wanting to get her attention. But really, what was the point? She wasn't going to open the door, and he wasn't inclined to argue through a one-inch-thick piece of wood.

What he needed to do was get in that bathroom. Right. No problem.

He cast one quick look back toward the bathroom door, but when Ella didn't fling it open and apologize for being in a mood, he moved on. He hoisted one leg over the windowsill and slipped back out onto the fire escape. The bathroom window was just to the right, but unfortunately there was no grating underneath it. Still, if he balanced on the railing and leaned over, he should be able to lift the window then climb through without falling to the alley below.

Fortunately he knew one thing for certain about Ella, and that was that she hardly ever remembered to close the bathroom window. The space was too small and the steam too intense for the long showers she coveted. He'd called her on it at least a dozen times, citing the possibility that someone would break in, and she'd remember to close it for a day or two before she slid back into her bad habit.

If he thought about this hard enough, he could probably talk himself out of it. After all, he was an attorney, not a gymnast. But it wasn't the dangers that were taking precedence in his mind, it was Ella.

That wasn't a situation he intended to let continue. He wanted her on his team. They *were* a team. And he was determined to tell her that—right now. If he waited for Ella to come out voluntarily, he might as well call from Texas. He loved her, but he had no illusions about her. Ella could sulk with the best of them. And if she'd decided she was pissed off, then she was capable of staying pissed off for hours.

Which meant that he really didn't have a choice.

He propped the flashlight on the railing, its beam aimed at the area beside the window. It provided enough light so that he could see what he was doing, and he was thankful for small favors. He leaned over as far as he could, grabbed the bottom of the window and slowly pushed it up. The oil he'd recently applied did the trick, and it rose smoothly and silently. If Ella was looking the other way, he was in business. And even if she was watching the window rise, she'd only sneak out into the other room. It wasn't as if she'd shove him off the window.

At least, he didn't think she would.

He swung a leg over the railing, followed by the other, so that he was sitting on the metal ledge. Next he grabbed hold of the piping that ran vertically along the building. He kept a tight grip for balance as he leaned forward, moving slowly until his fingers caught the window ledge. Then he pushed off so that both hands were on the ledge and his feet were pressed against the fire escape. Mentally he counted three, then hoisted himself up, using all the strength in his arms to pull him up and into the window.

A tight fit, but he made it. He slid through the opening, collapsed in a heap on the floor, then looked up to find Ella staring at him from the bathtub, her expression a mix of amusement and irritation.

"If you needed to go that bad, I'm sure Marjorie would have let you use her bathroom."

"We need to talk."

She grimaced, then nodded to the toilet as she pulled a towel off the rack and draped it over her, soaking the cloth but covering her more effectively than the smattering of bubbles.

He sat just inches from her, his fingers desperate to touch her. He knew better, though, than to try.

"What happened, El? I thought—" He closed his mouth, not sure what he'd thought. That they'd been having fun? That he'd made her see the light and she'd break up with Tony in the morning? That they'd live happily ever after? Unsure which to say, he finally settled on, "I thought we were having fun."

"Fun." She echoed the word. Not a question, not even a statement. Just an echo. The flatness of her voice surprised him. But the anger reflected in her eyes shocked the hell out of him. "You set me up, you son of a bitch."

Her words hit him with the force of a slap, and from the way she'd tightened her hand on the side of the tub, a real slap might be imminent, too.

He didn't deny it. How could he deny the truth?

"Just having fun? Just acting in the moment? Nothing that has to change our friendship? For God's sake, Shane, did you think I wouldn't ultimately figure it out?"

"Figure what out?" he shot back, the words coming out before he could censor his tongue. "That I'm in love with you?" It was too late to stop himself now, so he continued, "God, Ella, I hoped you *would* figure it out. I've been hoping you'd figure it out for months."

She just sat there for a moment and then her forehead crinkled, and he saw her shoulders sag a bit, as if his words were totally unexpected. "Love me?" She shook her head slowly. "You think you love me? Is that why you tricked me?"

"Tricked you? Is that how you see this?"

"This whole evening. The dinner, the candles, the condom all ready to go in your pocket. The whole thing. We didn't just act on the spur of the moment. You planned this. You planned and plotted and you flat-out lied to me and made me think it was all organic, just two friends looking at each other in a different light."

She was right, of course. He had lied. But he'd told himself he'd lied for a good cause—love. Now he needed to tell her that and make her understand. From the expression on her face, though, he wasn't sure that was going to be easy.

"I think being in love *is* taking a friendship to a new level."

"You're a bastard, Shane, you know that?" But the words lacked force, and when she tilted her head back against the side of the tub, she seemed defeated.

"How? How am I a bastard if all I'm doing is loving you?"

"Because you set out to seduce me knowing I'm in love with another man. And you risked our friendship to do it." She ran her fingers through her hair. "God, Shane. Don't you know that I need you in my life? I need to be able to count on you as a friend. I need you there for me, steady and real and everything you've always been."

"I can't be that man, Ella. I'm sorry if I knocked your perfectly ordered world out of kilter, but you can't get married to Tony just because you think he'll give you what you want. Not if you don't really love him."

"I *do* love him," she said fiercely.

Shane ignored her and went on. "You can't keep our friendship on hold, either. Not if it needs to grow. I did take a risk, you're right." He drew in a deep breath. "I risked our friendship for love. Because the truth is, El, I think you're worth it."

ELLA WASN'T SURE WHICH emotion was stronger. Anger, desire, fear. Shane thought she was worth it, but was she? Were they? Yes, Shane's touch drove her wild, but sex alone wasn't enough.

She wanted to lash out at him some more in anger,

but the brutal truth was that she wasn't so much angry as confused and scared. Flattered that he wanted her so badly but terrified of losing even one piece of the life that she'd put together so carefully. "You're my best friend, Shane. I love you, you know that. But please don't ask me to make our friendship into something else."

"Our friendship already is something else."

She closed her eyes, fighting back tears, everything she'd feared coming to fruition. Had it really been less than twenty-four hours since she'd had that fantasy about Shane in the library? How could so much have happened in so short a time?

"We love each other," she admitted. "We do. But as friends. And so help me, we're damn good together in bed. But heat isn't enough. Don't you get it? Love is about more than just heat. With Tony I have a whole life, a family. A whole future laid out for me." That was why people got married. For the fairy tale and the happily ever after. It's what she wanted more than anything, and it was what Tony could give her.

"Except that you *don't* love Tony," he said, his words stinging as sharply as ice.

"Of course I do!"

"No, El, you don't. You love the idea of Tony and you love Leah and Matty, but you don't love him. Not like that. Not like you love me."

"Dammit, Shane!" Her temper flared. "You're so damn arrogant. And you don't have any right—"

"Yes, I do. I'm your best friend. I have every right in the world to save you from the worst mistake of your life."

"I'm warning you, Shane. You're walking a fine line. Keep talking and you're going to regret it. We both are. I love Tony, and that's final."

"So you say, but what you really love is his family."

"Yes!" she screamed before she could censor her words. "Yes, that's part of it. I'll admit it. So what's wrong with that? There's no one else, *no one,* who can give me that. You sure as hell can't." He flinched a little at that, but he had to know it was true. After all, his family rivaled hers for lack of warm fuzzies.

"We can make our own family, El. A *real* family, the kind we want. Not the kind we were born into. And not one you decided to cling to because you were afraid of growing old alone." He drew in a breath. "I want you, El. I want *us.* And I want to make this work."

"Those are just words, Shane. What about action? Are you planning to stay here in New York? With me?"

"You know I can't do that."

She licked her lips, realizing only then that she'd been willing him to say yes. "I don't want a long-distance family, Shane," she whispered. "Tony's real and he's here and he's now."

"El, I have to take this job. You know that."

A rope of anger whipped through her. "So you want me but on your terms. Gee, that reminds me of someone. Who could it be? Oh yeah, my mom." She spat the last word, unable to stop the tears from streaming down her face. "She wanted a kid but only when it was convenient. Like when she needed to parade me around to show her clients what a great mommy she was."

"That's not fair," he said, his voice so soft and reasonable that it absolutely infuriated her.

"No, you're right. It's incredibly unfair. But it's the truth, and I have to live with it every day of my life."

"Dammit, El, if I stayed, would that be enough? Would you tell Tony it's over? Would you stay with me?"

She thought about calling his bluff, but he deserved an honest answer. She shook her head, the motion barely perceptible. "No. I'm sorry. No."

She couldn't stay there any longer. She stood up, the towel heavy and dripping water. He'd seen her naked, but he hadn't really seen her vulnerable as she was now, and she took great care to slip her robe on without him seeing any skin. She moved across the floor, leaving a trail of water, then headed straight for the front door.

She unlocked it and moved out into the hall, closing the door behind her. Her chest was so tight, she could barely breathe, and she leaned against the wall, sucking in air and telling herself she'd done the right thing. And she had. Of course she had.

One minute passed, then another, then another. She kept expecting the door to open and Shane to storm into the hall and demand to talk to her, just as he'd crawled in through the window. Despite her mood, the memory brought a smile to her face. She had to give the guy credit; he was definitely going all out. And apparently he knew when to stop, too. They'd needed the confrontation in the bathroom, she knew that. She'd gone to hide when really she should have just had it out with him.

Now she wasn't hiding. They'd said it all. Now she was stewing. And Shane knew her well enough to understand that she needed to be left alone.

Would Tony understand those little quirks?

She frowned at the uninvited question. Of course he would. She'd known Shane for close to twenty years. It just made sense that he already knew. Tony would catch up in time.

And Shane just had to realize that's the way it was. She'd found her mate, and it wasn't Shane.

She didn't stay outside as long as he'd expected, and when she came back in, her face was set. Her professional expression. His gut twisted. This was the look of a woman about to walk into an oral examination, not a woman about to greet the love of her life.

"I'm sorry I ran out," she said. "We should probably talk."

"I want you," he said. Abrupt maybe. But what else was there to say?

"I want you, too," she said, but not with the tone he longed for. And as the seconds passed, he felt more and more desolate.

"Just tell me what you came back in to say, Ella. We might as well get through this quickly."

She flinched as if he'd slapped her, and he wanted to put his arms around her and comfort her. But he was the last person she'd want to take comfort from right then. He'd been the one to push them to the breaking point, he knew that. And maybe he should have never even broached the subject. But that would have meant living the rest of his life as a lie, pretending he felt less than he did every time he saw or spoke to Ella.

He supposed he could have just eased out of her life without any real explanation. But that would have hurt both of them. At least this way he was being honest.

And what really burned his butt was that Ella wasn't meeting him halfway; she wasn't being honest. Unfortunately he couldn't just put her on the stand and cross-examine the truth out of her. He had to wait for Ella to admit the truth herself…if she ever did.

At the moment, though, she wasn't saying anything. "Ella?" he prompted.

She'd been looking down, and now she tilted her head just enough so that he could see the hint of tears clinging to her lashes. Again he felt the impulse to take her in his arms, but right now he was in limbo, neither friend nor lover. He kept his feet glued to the spot.

"We're good together, Shane. In and out of bed, we're good."

She was saying the right words, but he knew her well enough to recognize this speech wasn't going to end well. His body tensed as he mentally predicted where she'd go next, while hoping like hell he was wrong.

"But I'm with Tony. You know I am."

"So you've told me."

Her face flushed, her temper obviously flaring. "Dammit, Shane, don't you see? You're my *best* friend. What if we started dating and it all fell apart? How could we salvage it? If I lose you—" She closed her mouth, turning abruptly from him as if she'd said too much.

He wanted to shake her and tell her she was being absurd. Even more, he wanted to shake her mother for giving Ella material goods but not giving her anything she actually needed.

He forced himself to stay level and reasonable, not to sound accusatory. But he needed to know. He really, really needed to know. "Do you truly believe you love Tony? That you can love him for the rest of your life?"

"I'm going to marry him, Shane," she said. "Don't insult me by asking that again."

He cringed, but nodded.

"Look," she said, leaning forward and putting her head in her hands, "you know how important you are to me. How important our friendship is. I don't want to ruin that. You promised this thing between us wouldn't screw it all up."

He took a deep breath, not wanting to say it but owing her the truth. "I'm sorry, El. I meant it when I said it, but now…well, I think I lied."

"What?"

"Everything's changed now. And, yeah, I did that. I came here tonight planning to win you over, just as I'd win a court case. I admit that. I had my evidence, my props—hell, I even made up those damn stories. Took three days and a hell of a lot of wine, but I did it because I needed to get through to you. Somehow I was going to make you see."

"You wrote—"

"But I knew going in that I could lose and Tony could win. I could live with that. And now it's happened. I lost. First time I've lost a case, and it's the first time it's been truly important to me." He drew in a breath, determined to keep his voice steady. "But you lose, too, Ella. I may be losing the love of my life, but you're losing your best friend."

"What are you talking about—*no*." She shook her head. "Shane, no. Don't do this to me."

Her eyes filled with tears, and his resolve wavered. But he knew he had to do this. There wasn't a middle ground here. He couldn't hover in the distance, the best friend that the husband didn't trust. The one who had the hots for the wife. He couldn't be that man.

"You're the best friend I ever had, Ella. And I doubt anyone can ever be a better one. But I told you tonight that our friendship had changed." He moved to the door, opened it. "You'll survive just fine without me. I'm not your only close friend anymore. And, you know, if all else fails, you can talk it over with Tony."

"You son of a bitch." Cold shock had painted her face, and the words came out an icy whisper. "So it's choose you or lose you?"

"Yeah. That about sums it up."

And then he stepped over the threshold and into the hall. He started down the stairs, expecting to hear her calling after him. But she didn't.

He hit the fifth-floor landing and paused, closing his eyes and exhaling. Because he couldn't quite believe that he'd just walked away from Ella, from the woman he loved.

Even more, he couldn't believe he'd lost her.

12

ELLA STARED AT THE DOOR, feeling shell-shocked and not at all sure whether she should cry or— She frowned, realizing that there was no "or." Crying was the best and only option.

No.

She needed to pull herself together. She needed to focus on the fact that she'd made the right decision and that she would get through this.

She needed to talk.

The irony, of course, was that she needed to talk to her best friend, and he was now pounding the pavement. He had a lot of walking to do to get back to his apartment, because the power was still out, which meant the subways weren't running.

Well, that was fine. She could just find someone else to talk to. And with anger fueling her every move, she dug in her purse for her cell phone. She'd turned it off after Tony had called, and now she turned it back on. One bar of juice left. That would probably be enough.

She punched in the number, tapping her foot while she waited to hear a voice at the other end of the line. As soon as she did, she sagged in relief, then immediately stiffened in horror as she realized who she'd called—and what it meant that she'd called Leah instead of Tony.

"Hello?" Leah's perky tone filtered through the phone, but Ella barely heard her. Instead she slammed the phone shut and tried to catch her breath. For half a second she considered dialing back. The truth was, Leah was a good friend. And even though she was Tony's sister, Ella could trust Leah to shoot straight with her. More, Ella knew that Leah would be there for Ella even if Tony wasn't.

With a frown she flipped open the phone again and dialed. Not Leah but another friend. Funny that, despite everything, Shane had been right. He might have been her best friend, but he wasn't her only one. She did have other confidantes. And right now she really hoped that Ronnie was answering her phone.

BRUNO LOUNGED ON THE COUCH, his droopy eyes never leaving Shane and his tail thumping a rhythm against the overstuffed pillow. Normally Bruno wasn't allowed on the sofa. That he was comfortably settled there now was testament to how distracted Shane was.

He had to get out of there. Not easy when there

was no power, but there wasn't any point in staying. He needed to get in a car, get on a plane, somehow get the hell out of Dodge. All his work was wrapped up in Manhattan, but there was a truckful of case files on his desk in Houston. If he could just get down there, he could lose himself in the work. And maybe if he was lucky, he'd forget that his heart was broken.

He moved into the kitchen and pulled open the fridge, withdrawing a lukewarm beer and popping the top. The sun was barely up, but he didn't care and he took two long swallows, then raised the glass to Bruno. "You're going to like Houston, boy. You'll have a yard. Your own little square of grass. Canine heaven."

Bruno whined, and Shane tipped his head at the dog. "My sentiments exactly."

Since there wasn't any point in standing around feeling sorry for himself, he went to his closet for his suitcase. There was no way he could finish packing up in just a few hours, but his subtenant wasn't moving in for another month. He could get down to Houston, then come back for his stuff in a week or so.

The task force had access to a private jet, and considering the amount of work being generated, he imagined that it was currently cooling its rudders at LaGuardia, just waiting for the blackout to lift or the backup generators to provide enough juice to authorize clearance. All he needed to do was call his boss, get a seat on that plane, con Danny into watching Bruno for a few days, then head to the airport to wait.

Not a perfect plan but better than getting drunk in his tomb of an apartment.

And on that upbeat note he picked up his bag and started to pack.

RONNIE LEANED BACK AGAINST the wooden kitchen chair, a warm Diet Coke open in her hand. "Wow. You really had a busy night."

"Very funny." Ella took a sip from her own soda can, then made a face at the temperature. "What am I going to do? He was right. Shane was absolutely right. I'm more in love with Tony's family than with Tony."

She still couldn't believe that she'd dialed Leah instead of Tony. He was supposed to be her soul mate, the love of her life, the man she was going to marry.

"Just because you called Leah doesn't mean you don't love Tony. I mean, you *were* planning to discuss your relationship with another man. No one would fault you for not bringing Tony into the loop on that one."

"I told myself that, too," Ella said. "But it was a lie. Same as all the times I've said I'm in love with Tony. It wasn't just that I didn't immediately want to call him, it's that it didn't really matter to me if he was even there *to* call. Does that make sense?"

"A little."

"Matty and Leah are great. We have so much fun. And I have all these fantasies about us with our kids and grandkids around the Christmas tree years and years from now. And you know what? Shane's always there, too."

"And Tony?"

"I usually remember about halfway through the fantasy and have him walk in carrying eggnog or something." She brushed a hand under her eye, surprised to find her cheek dry. She'd cried so much the past hour, it just seemed natural to find her cheeks wet. "I do love Tony, but not like that. He's a sweet, honorable, good man. But..." She trailed off with a shrug, then looked at Ronnie, sure her eyes were pleading. "Why the hell couldn't I have realized this before? Why did it take sleeping with Shane—and Shane walking out—for me to realize?"

"Because you want it easy," Ronnie said with a shrug. "You want the fairy tale. But it doesn't always work out that way. Sometimes it's really messy."

"You're talking like a professor."

Ronnie laughed. "Sorry."

She ran her fingers through her hair. "You're right, though. I thought I could have it all. My perfect friend Shane. My perfect husband with the perfect family. I saw it all as perfect because all the pieces were there. But take Shane out of the equation, and I'm suddenly forced to see the real picture."

"A very astute analysis."

Ella frowned, not feeling particularly astute. "What do I do now?"

"You tell Tony," Ronnie said. "Tell him before he gives you a ring. You owe him that."

She nodded. "I know. I'd already thought of that. I meant what do I do about Shane?"

"Go after him."

"He tricked me."

"He knocked some sense into you."

She grimaced. "He knocked me, all right."

Ronnie's mouth curved into a small grin. "You're doing the right thing."

"It still scares me. I want the package Tony comes with. Shane's just like me. His family's a mess. It would just be us. Just the two of us against the world."

"And your friends. Jack and I aren't going anywhere, and I bet Matty and Leah aren't either."

Ronnie was right. She may have come to New York without a family, but she had one now. Not by blood but just as strong.

"And you'll have kids, too."

Ella blinked, thinking suddenly about being pregnant, carrying Shane's child. Of picnics in the park with a baby on a blanket. Maybe another one toddling through the grass.

"Start our own family," she said simply.

"Why not? You both made your own life. Who better qualified than the two of you?" Ronnie reached across the table and grabbed her hands, giving them a squeeze. "And wouldn't you rather have *your* family? Not one that you squeezed into?"

"I can't go back to Texas."

"I think you can do whatever you set your mind to," Ronnie said.

Ella shook her head, and on this one point she was unmovable. "Not that. I can't. Not to live, anyway."

"So you visit. He's only there to get the firm started, right?"

Ella nodded. "Then he's supposed to get a transfer to D.C." She made a face. D.C. was not on her list of favorite cities, but it was heaven on earth for Shane, who wanted to do all sorts of legal work that was tied to the government.

"Could you live there?"

"Sure," she said automatically, then realized it was true. If it was important to Shane, she could do it. "I mean, they have museums there, too, right?"

Ronnie's smile was almost maternal, even though they weren't that many years apart in age. "That they do."

Ella sighed. "The thing is, I can picture a future without Tony. Without New York. But I can't picture one without Shane." She sighed. "I should have listened to you yesterday morning."

"Probably true," Ronnie said with a grin. "What brilliant thing did I say?"

"About how marriage is about being yourself, only more. I'm not myself with Tony. But I am with Shane."

"Don't tell me," Ronnie said. She nodded toward the door. "Go tell *him.*"

SHE COULDN'T FIND HIM. She pounded on the door, but nothing. Then she pressed her ear against the wood, listening for the clack of Bruno's toenails against the battered hardwood. Nothing.

He must be out walking the dog.

She considered waiting—after all, how long could it take?—but she couldn't bear it. So she headed back down the elevator. The elderly doorman, Max, had been busy helping one of the tenants when she'd arrived, but now he smiled at her. "Miss Ella. Good to see you. You getting something outta Shane's apartment?"

"I was hoping to get Shane."

"Ah, well. You missed him by about an hour." He looked at his watch. "No, it's goin' on two hours now."

"Two? Is he walking Bruno?"

"Be a long walk to Texas," Max said.

A chill settled over Ella, and she reached out and took the old man's hand. "Max, what exactly are you talking about?"

"Decided to leave a day early. Took the dog and a suitcase and got into a taxi. Streets still aren't that clear, but he didn't seem to care."

"He's taking a taxi to Texas?"

"To LaGuardia. Guess them government attorneys got access to some nice private jets."

"He's leaving." She said the words more to herself than to Max, but the doorman patted her shoulder.

"Now, now. He's coming back in a few weeks. Still has to make arrangements for the rest of his stuff. Left in a hurry. Work, he said. Must've been important, too. Never seen his face so serious." The doorman shrugged. "I imagine he's either in the air by now or sitting in a lounge in LaGuardia waiting for clearance."

"Right. Thanks."

She headed outside to the little courtyard that filled the space between the street and the building's entrance. She took a seat on a stone bench and pulled out her cell phone, turning it over in her hand. She should have called first, but the phone was so low on juice, she hadn't wanted to risk having no battery if she had an emergency.

No. That was a lie. She hadn't called because she'd been afraid he'd tell her not to come. Now she wished she'd called and begged.

She couldn't believe he'd really left for Texas. And without saying goodbye.

Except he had said goodbye. They'd said their goodbyes, however unpleasant, in her bathroom. And now she was kicking herself for that.

With a sigh she stood up. Nothing to do now but head back to her apartment. When the power returned, she could charge up her phone. Call his cell. Maybe catch him at the airport. She'd wanted to talk in person, but she could grovel over the phone if she had to.

That he'd left so quickly, though, made her wonder if groveling would do any good at all. She may have already blown it, and the realization made her queasy.

She headed down the street, not paying attention to where she was going. Just walking. After a few minutes, though, she realized that her feet had taken her to a nearby park, the one where they used to come to walk Bruno. And the one where they'd once seen the couple making out under the tree.

Not where she wanted to be right now, and she started to turn away to walk in the opposite direction.

That was when she heard it—a deep and familiar bark. She frowned, sure her mind was playing tricks, but she walked toward the sound anyway.

And then, as she rounded the curve, the dog run came into view and there was Bruno, romping on the grass. And there stood Shane, leaning against a railing, looking out toward the river, his suitcase beside him.

And right then her heart just about stopped in her chest. She forced herself to walk forward, even though she was seeing the scene through vision blurred by tears.

The power was still off, and the city seemed unusually quiet, the streets flooded with more bicycles than cars. She hurried toward him, dodging a woman on a mountain bike, then slowed as she got near, wondering if he'd sense her presence and turn.

He didn't, but Bruno did, barking a greeting as she moved past the run. Shane turned at the sound of the bark, his expression at first curious and then, when he saw her, guarded.

"I'm sorry," she said, and it was as if she'd flipped a switch. The ice in his eyes melted, the warmth marred by only the slightest hint of a shadow.

"What exactly are you sorry for?"

She swallowed. "I'm sorry we fought. And I'm sorry I pushed you away. And I'm sorry you went six months without being able to tell me you loved me."

The shadow faded, replaced with a rare kind of joy. She grinned, her own heart melting.

"I couldn't stay here," he said. "Not without you in my life. I was heading out of the city. It's a miracle I'm not gone already."

"I know. Max told me." She frowned. "Why aren't you gone?"

"Fate maybe? Danny wasn't able to watch Bruno. I took him to the kennel, but they were shut down. We came here instead. Bruno needed to burn off some energy. He'd had a rather lonely twenty-four hours."

"Shane, I—"

But he just pressed a finger to her lips. "Later. Right now just tell me one thing—what about Tony?"

"Tony's okay," she said. "But he's not you. And he's not for me."

He stared at her for a minute, then smiled, slow and wide and a little bit smug. "Told you so."

She couldn't help it. She laughed. "Yeah, you did."

They spent an hour in the park, not talking about what had happened but not avoiding it either. Just playing. Walking and chatting and tossing sticks for Bruno. She sensed Shane still needed to absorb the turn of events.

When they got ready to head back, she went for broke. She cocked her head toward the single tree that towered over the park. The tree where they'd seen the couple making out so many years ago.

"Wanna try?" she asked, a tease in her voice. "A bit more daring than a fire escape, don't you think?"

He didn't answer with words, just pulled her over toward the tree and pushed her up against it. The bark was scratchy even through her shirt, but when his mouth closed over hers, she forgot all about the discomfort. Behind him Bruno whined, eager to go home.

Like a man possessed, Shane attacked her mouth, sliding his hands up her shirt to play with her breasts. "What do you want?"

"I already told you," she said. "Only you."

"Good answer," he said. "But what about now? Right now."

"Whatever it takes," she said. "Whatever it takes to get back in your good graces."

"Really?" His brow raised, and he had a devious expression in his eyes. Oh yeah, it was going to be okay between them. "I want to make love to you."

"Here?"

"Would you let me if I said yes?"

She hesitated, thinking about the people on the streets and the sun in the sky. "Yeah," she finally said.

"Another good answer. I think you're on a roll." He kissed her—hard—then backed off, taking her hand. "But you don't really want to do it. Not here."

"No," she admitted.

"I know you, El. I know you better than anyone."

She nodded. "I know. And I love that." She took a deep breath. "Shane, I love you, too."

"You could have told me that in your apartment," he said, grabbing his suitcase.

She shook her head, taking Bruno's leash as they

walked back to his apartment. "I needed a reality check. So I guess I should thank you."

"I like that better than you calling me a bastard."

"Well, you *were*."

"I was desperate," he said. "And blinded by love."

She smiled up at him. "I know the feeling."

"So what do we do now?" he asked.

"I'm going to call Tony. It won't be easy, but I need to do it now." She drew in a breath and faced him. "And you're going to Texas."

The corner of his mouth curved up. "I am?"

"Well, not today. But Monday, just as you planned. You can't walk away from an opportunity like that. And by the time you get the transfer to D.C., I'll be done with grad school. And in the meantime…" She shrugged. "I guess we'll rack up the frequent-flier miles."

He laughed, but his expression quickly turned serious. "And what about D.C.? You hate D.C."

"I do," she said. "But I love you more."

"Oh, Ella." They'd reached his door, and he paused just long enough to kiss her, long and deep.

The kiss knocked her a little sideways, the ground seeming to shift beneath her. She smiled to herself, and Shane noticed.

"What?"

"Just reality shifting," she said.

"A good shift?"

"Perfect," she said.

Once they'd walked into the apartment, he took her hand, touching her as if he had to make up for lost time. "What made you change your mind?" he asked, helping her peel off her top.

Her fingers closed on a button of his shirt. "I guess I just finally opened my eyes. I don't just want a lover, I want a friend."

"And a family?"

"Well, I was kind of thinking we could maybe start one of our own. Unless that scares you away," she asked as she undid the last button.

"The only thing that scares me is not having you."

"Then you have nothing to be afraid of."

With a little *pop* the power came back on, the light from the overhead lamp flooding the room. Ella looked around, her brows lifting and a smile coming automatically to her mouth.

"What?" he asked.

"I was just wondering if everything would feel different once the magic of the blackout was over."

"Does it?"

"Yeah," she said, tackling the button and zipper of his jeans. "It feels perfect."

With both hands he pushed her pants down, so that she was standing in front of him wearing only panties. He slipped a hand between her legs, and once again she felt lit up.

"So what do you want to do?" he asked.

"Honestly? I want to sleep. With you next to me. And I want to wake up in your arms and…" She trailed off meaningfully.

"I like the sound of that 'and.'"

She laughed and led him to bed, this friend she'd always known and now saw in a whole new light. "I love you, Shane Walker. I think I always have."

He kissed her neck, then spooned her, just where he belonged. "Believe me, sweetheart," he said, his voice a whisper of breath on her ear. "I know exactly what you mean."

THE SECRET DIARY

**A new drama unfolds for six
of the state's wealthiest bachelors.**

This newest installment continues with

LESS-THAN-INNOCENT INVITATION

by Shirley Rogers

(Silhouette Desire #1671)

Melissa Mason will do almost anything
to avoid talking to her former fiancé,
Logan Voss. Too bad his ranch is the
only place she can stay while in Royal.
What's worse, he seems determined
to renew their acquaintance...
in every way.

Available August 2005 at your favorite retail outlet.

If you enjoyed what you just read,
then we've got an offer you can't resist!

Take 2 bestselling
love stories FREE!

Plus get a FREE surprise gift!